Katharina Marcus

Eleanor McGraw, a pony named Mouse and a boy called Fire

ISBN-10: 149031234X

ISBN-13: 978-1490312347

Chapter 1

For a fraction within eternity she didn't know who, what or where she was. She was floating in a soup of grey, wondering whether she was an embryo in a womb or a mammoth tree, a thousand years old.

With the question of age came the realisation that she was a who, not a what, and with the who came a name. Eleanor.

My name is Eleanor.

I am a human.

I am 13 years old.

I am in bed.

It's supposed to be my bed but it smells wrong.

It doesn't smell like home. It smells of paint. And dentist.

If I open my eyes (but I don't want to) I will see white walls, thick yellow curtains (a gift from Granny), a perfectly polished wooden floor, a dark red rug (still not sure about the colour), a brand new wardrobe (which I chose), a brand new desk (which I chose) and my old rickety desk lamp (which I love). There are two unpacked boxes of books at the foot of the bed and an unassembled bookshelf leaning against the wall (can't be bothered). I...

There was a gentle tap on the door and suddenly she knew that this was the second knock. It had been the first one, a while back, which had dragged her into consciousness through that opaque liquid of raw thought matter. Still, she didn't react.

She kept her eyes closed and looked through the door from behind her eyelids. She could see Kjell's silhouette standing patiently on the other side. He waited for another few seconds for her to answer then silently moved off. This was what set this man apart from the Jerrys, Micks and Lukes of this world. The JMLs would have just walked in anyway or, most likely, not knocked in the first place. Eleanor liked him for this. For the respect he showed her and the quiet reassurance, with which he went about his day. *'Shame,'* she heard her grandmother giggle in the ether, *'it comes with such utter dullness.'*

She was beginning to find it difficult to keep her eyes shut now.

She took a deep breath and opened them.

It was odd.

Everything was just as she had seen it from inside her skull yet somehow, in reality, it wasn't half as stark. The sun fell through the curtains and the whole room was bathed in a golden glow. There was her amply furnished pin board above her desk opposite the bed and pictures up, which they had hung the night before, along with the guitar swing that was now waiting for her to liberate the instrument from its travel case.

It was alright.

There was a noise from under the door and she turned her head to see an envelope being pushed into the room.

A beat, shuffling footsteps, then murmuring voices on the landing. A kiss *(did she actually hear that or just imagine it?)*, heavy footsteps back to the master bedroom and lighter ones down the stairs, carrying a suitcase. The front door opened and shut.

She really needed a pee now but didn't want her mother to find out she was awake and had chosen not to say goodbye.

Why, anyway? Why didn't I just go and say bye? He's off to Sweden for a fu-ne-ral, for heaven's sake.

It was a rhetorical question that didn't even sound like her own voice in her head. She knew the answer. It lay somewhere between feeling awkward around this softly spoken, intelligent and successful foreigner and being the outsider to an emerging bubble of a happy, brand new life.

A remnant of old.

A child of the JMLs.

Chapter 2

"So, what shall we do with our Thursday then? How do you fancy a bike ride to those fields we saw from the car the other day and explore the countryside around here? Or we could cycle to the beach and eat ice cream."

Her mum was propped up in bed, balancing a mug of Ovaltine on her enormous belly. Eleanor gave her a sceptical look.

"Are you sure you should still be riding a bike, mum? Our baby is due in five weeks, two days and Kjell would kill me if something happened to you two while he's gone. If he had his way you'd stay right where you are and I'd wait on you hand and foot. And I'm not sure he doesn't have a point."

Her mum laughed.

"Firstly, *my* baby is due in five weeks and two days, *your* little brother or sister. I didn't realise you were counting, by the way, that's cute. And secondly, like you quite rightly pointed out, Kjell is not here. Seriously," she dropped her voice and looked straight at Eleanor, her often unsteady hazel eyes suddenly focusing sharply, "I'll be fine. - Why? What was in that envelope?"

"A death threat," Eleanor dead-panned, "No, a load of cash for me to use for cabs and stuff in an emergency and a whole list of phone numbers where I can call him should I not get through on his mobile. He's worried, mum. Why is he so worried?"

Her mum laughed again, running her free hand through the mass of shaggy dark brown hair she was forever trying to smooth down with little success. She held it in the nape of her neck, arm resting on her head, as she sighed deeply, while her gaze wandered to just above Eleanor's shoulder, staring into the distance beyond the walls.

"He's not worried, babe, he's being practical," a wry smile spread across her face before her eyes fixed on Eleanor again, "There are lots of men like that. It's just that he's the first one of those you have met, thanks to my appalling track record. Also, it's his first child. It's different for him."

"What do you mean?"

"Well, I got all my fretting out of my system with you and now I know that a child can be so skinny and tiny it disappears when you shut one eye, yet still navigate safely through all sorts of chaos and make it to nearly fourteen relatively unharmed."

"Hm."

Eleanor had only been half listening and had dropped her head to start cleaning imaginary dirt from under her fingernails. Isabel sipped on her drink, searching her daughter's forehead over the rim of the mug.

"What do you mean 'hm'?"

"Nothing. - Just hm. So, you sure about this bike ride?"

"Yep."

"Ok. Bike ride then," Eleanor looked up again, "But I vote countryside. There is only so much beach and ice cream I can handle in one week."

"Shame. I was looking forward to the ice cream part," Isabel released her hair and shuffled into a more upright position, "Now what's the 'hm' about?"

Eleanor could feel her mum probing around in her brain and sighed because she knew, she knew and wouldn't let it go.

"It's about Monday, isn't it? You're anxious. - Look, we can postpone you going there till after the holidays, if you like. Settle in a bit more. Get your bearings. You finished your year in Gloucester. You don't have to go back to school here now, just have an extra week's holiday," she finished on a laugh, "I would."

Yes, I know. But chances of me suddenly growing a foot or so over the summer and putting on a stone or two are pretty slim (no pun intended), so why bother? Might as well get it over and done with now.

She didn't say it though. She didn't want to discuss it. So she shook her head in a deliberately absentminded fashion, knowing full well it wouldn't wash with her mum but hoping that she would accept the farce for what it was and let her change the subject.

"Mum, do you miss Gloucester? Do you miss our - chaos?" Eleanor asked.

"Not yet, no. Do you?"

"Maybe. I don't know. Everything is so, so, so tidy in this house. And everything smells of dentist all the time. It doesn't feel like home. I miss my bed, I miss the colours. I miss the smell of other people."

"Roll ups and beer you mean? Come here, gimme a cuddle," her mum's face went soft and serious as she put her arm around Eleanor and kissed her on the top of the head, "hmm, sprite hair, lovely. – Look, if you want to paint your walls pea green with orange and canary yellow zebra stripes, feel free. If you want to get rid of the bed and put a mattress on the floor, feel free. This is your house, too," after a moment she added with a grin, "If you want to start smoking and drinking though don't feel free, feel decidedly unfree and shackled."

Eleanor ignored the last remark.

"No, it's not. It's Kjell's."

"No, it's *our* house. In very real terms, we bought it together."

"But he picked it," Eleanor found herself arguing *(why am I even going on about this?)*, "he's been living here for months."

"Only so you didn't have to change schools half way through the year, hon," her mum's voice took on a no-nonsense, mildly annoyed tone, "A lot of this move has revolved around you and your feelings, Eleanor. We've tried to do it all as smoothly as possible for your benefit, you know."

It didn't revolve around my feelings! It revolved around what you assumed my feelings would be! We 'discussed' it but you never actually asked outright! And anyway since when do you care about taking me out of school half way through the year?!

Although screaming inside, Eleanor knew that it was up to her how the rest of this day would go and she didn't want to have a row. Instead, she snuggled into the hug again, snaking around the big belly between them and stated quietly, "I'm sorry. It's just, I think part of me misses them, you know. And I keep thinking, so must you. - It's so terribly, terribly quiet in this house."

"Sorry, you lost me, miss who?"

Her mum looked genuinely puzzled.

"Nobody," Eleanor sighed, "The JMLs."

"The what?"

"The Jerrys, Micks and Lukes of this world."

Suddenly the mount of flesh next to her started trembling and then bouncing wildly until she was practically catapulted out of the hug. She sat upright and looked at her mum wide-eyed.

Her mum was laughing so hard, tears had formed in the corners of her eyes. Once she had calmed down a little, her eyes narrowed and she looked inquisitively into Eleanor's.

"Ok, who came up with that? You or your grandma? Be honest."

Eleanor swallowed.

"Part part. I shortened it."

Her mum drew a long breath.

"Right. Now. Listen. You're that age now - so if you remember nothing else, remember this: the JMLs", another giggle escaped Isabel's lips before she could continue, "of this world, the rock stars with the bikes and the guitars and the pet wood lice and the tattoos and the wild imagination and the music that burns itself into your soul and the words that never leave, they are fantastic fun and I don't regret a single day spent with any of them, particularly with your father. But you know, they are also incredibly self involved. It is all about them. About *their* chaos and *their* joy and *their* pain and *their* soul searches and *their* creativity and *their* self esteem or lack thereof. About what *they* want to eat and what *they* want to listen to and what *they* want to do next. I know your Grandma thinks, Kjell is boring. And I know you find him awkward because he doesn't come with this perpetual noise level that seems to have emanated from your collective father figures so far. But the fact is, for the first time in about twenty years, I am actually getting my own stuff done. And for the first time in my *life* I have somebody who calls me Isabel – not Izzy, not Bizzy, not Bella, not Lala, not Bumblebee but Isabel. I've got somebody who is genuinely interested in how I'm progressing with what I'm doing, who lets me breathe my own breaths and who wouldn't care if I was more successful than him. And not because he doesn't have his own things going on and needs to live through me, either. I've had that one before, too. No, because he is content enough in his own skin to let me be. I don't know whether you understand any of this yet but, look, go over to that chest of drawers and open the bottom drawer for me." Eleanor did as requested. "Now take out the black folder at the top and bring it here."

When Eleanor arrived back at the bed, her mum grabbed the folder and opened it. She took out some sheets of paper and shoved them into Eleanor's hands.

"Take a peek."

Eleanor found herself looking at music, handwritten in her mum's unmistakable stroke. As her eyes moved along the notes she started hearing a sweet, slow melody in her head

– an intro to something bigger and breathtaking yet distinctly simple.

"Wow, mum, I didn't realise you started composing again. This sounds great. Very sweet. When did you start doing this? What is it going to be?"

Isabel shrugged.

"To be honest, I'm not sure what it wants to be. I've been playing other people's music for so long.... I don't know. I think it might be for your brother or sister. Like *Kittens in the Den* was for you. Although this one," she poked her belly lovingly with a finger, "doesn't appear to be half as talented as you were. Seems more interested in sleeping and eating than composing. But that isn't the point. The point is, I started when we got here," she looked at Eleanor almost imploringly, "Somehow, this, Kjell, the silence, it works for me, you see? It's like, like I can finally hear my own notes again," she took the sheets from Eleanor and shuffled to get up, "Now, can we go cycling or is this conversation some elaborate ploy to keep me in bed after all? Let's roll."

Chapter 3

They had only been going for about ten minutes when Eleanor heard her mum holler from behind to stop. When she did and turned around she immediately started to regret having accepted the bike ride idea.

The exercise in the sweltering late morning heat had turned the walrus that was her heavily pregnant mother into a bright red blob creature, panting heavily and dripping with sweat.

"I need a rest, hon, I'm sorry."

Isabel got off her bike. She let it rest against a fence, took her helmet off, leant forward and lifted her shirt to mop her face, exposing the taut belly underneath. Just then, the baby decided to move and Eleanor could see it shifting under the skin. It made her heart quicken with a sudden jolt of anxiety and she began looking around frantically for a place where her mum could sit and rest in the shade for a bit.

They knew from the expedition earlier in the week that the road they were on was the main road into nowhere. There were a few more detached dwellings with manicured lawns on either side, then an open green on the right opposite a long, impenetrable and unkempt hedge of seven foot high bramble, elderberry and rosehip bushes, which had been fenced in with 'Private' signs nailed to the fence at regular intervals. Beyond that, where civilisation truly stopped, the road led through a small wooded area, on the other side of which were open fields and eventually a farm.

The wooded area had been where they had been headed but looking at her mum now, Eleanor was tempted to just walk up to the front door of any of the guaranteed-to-own-a-teapot houses and ask to utilise their gazebo. The scene in her mind made her giggle and her mum, who'd progressed to sipping water from a bottle now, frowned at her inquisitively. Eleanor waved off the question and looked around again. There appeared to be a shady gap between the 'Private' fence line and the flint stone wall encompassing the house just before it.

Eleanor squinted at it.

"Look mum, I think there is a twitten that goes up there. Let's see whether we can find a nice tree stump or something for you to sit on."

They pushed their bikes across the road and entered the path. Although the entrance was obscured by low hanging branches, once passed, the twitten turned out to be surprisingly wide. It was lined on one side by the same hedge that ran along the main road and on the other by the continuation of the flint stone wall, in front of which stood some sweet chestnut trees interlaced with hazels and shrubs, creating a dark, cool corridor under a canopy of leafy green.

Coming out of the glaring sun, both their eyes and bodies had to adjust and Eleanor felt a couple of shivers ripple through her body. They were only subtle but rather than ebb away, they seemed to lodge themselves in a state of suspended animation somewhere deep inside between her stomach and hips. They stayed there as she pushed on up the path, trying to ignore the very clear feeling that the decision to go in here had been one of those moments in life when it really *did* matter whether you went left or right. And she had no idea, whether in a good or a bad way.

Her mother, however, left no doubt as to her feelings about getting out of the sun and into the shade and kept making appreciative noises.

"Oh, this is much better. Well spotted, Eleanor. Oh look, there is actually a bench! How perfect is that?"

Only now did Eleanor notice a gap in the hedgerow ahead, making space for a long metal gate. Opposite the gate somebody had indeed dumped a park bench under a tree.

Her mum's legs suddenly went into overtime as she pushed past Eleanor and hurried towards it. She wedged her bike between the wall and a tree and flopped down, stretching out her feet.

"Ahhh," she exhaled, "wake me when it's home time." Eleanor followed her slowly, wondering not for the first time in her life, how it could possibly be that two people in the same place at the same time could perceive it so utterly differently. While her mum had clearly found an oasis of rest, in which all that was lacking was a handsome man feeding her grapes and massaging her feet, all Eleanor could feel was overwhelming loneliness seeping through the cool air. She felt almost as if she was back in the grey soup of pre-consciousness that had marked the beginning of this day, although this time the question was not who or what she was but *why* she was *still here*. Why she had not been taken *(where?)* with the others *(who?)*.

Amidst this strange sense of devastation, a fragment of a song that Jerry had used to play for her when she was little came into her head: *'There is no treasure left here; no joy no light, no gold; what once was bright and beautiful; is withered now and old; so don't go looking further, just turn around and run; back to the beginning, to where you started from.'*

Only she *couldn't* turn around.

Pulled along by an invisible thread, yet somehow dragged against the tide, she felt as if she was wading through treacle and if she had had to run, she wouldn't have been able to. The idea terrified her and she tried to calm herself by silently singing the lines again in her head. The attempt backfired because then, for a moment, she wasn't sure anymore whether she had maybe heard the music for real, ever so faintly, in the distance and that freaked her out even more.

When she finally sat down next to her mum on the bench, it felt like it had taken hours to get there.

11

"This is not a good place, mum. I don't like it. I reckon we should go back as soon as you can. Go home, have some ice tea, no more adventures."

"Teenagers," her mum mumbled, "you're so sensitive. - Why can't you just ignore the vibe and chill?" She opened her eyes and stared ahead at the metal gate. "We'll go in a minute. It does taste rather of sadness around here. – What do you reckon is in there?"

Eleanor shrugged.

"Something private," she answered dryly before getting up to have a look.

As she approached the gate, she knew that she was edging towards the source of whatever it was that was hanging in the air but strangely that came as a relief. With every step closer the feeling became less hers and more that of what lay beyond. She was half expecting to find an old cemetery and was genuinely surprised and mildly disappointed to find an empty plot of grazing land instead, the other side of which was not discernable from this vantage point.

"It's just an empty field, mum. I guess it normally has cows or sheep in it, I can see a barn or something."

"Not a cemetery then? Hm," Isabel grunted over from the bench.

Eleanor smiled and was about to turn back when suddenly there was a movement quite close to her, in the hedgerow adjoining the other side of the gate. She stepped onto the bottom rung to lean over - and suddenly found herself eye to eye with a pony.

It was small, a funny kind of blue-grey colour and was watching Eleanor with sorrowful eyes. As soon as Eleanor looked into them, she knew that she was facing the owner and occupant of that wasteland of grief she had just trudged through up the path.

"Hello there," Eleanor whispered softly and stretched out a hand, "I'm Eleanor. Pleased to meet you."

The pony hesitated then slowly came forward to nuzzle the palm of Eleanor's hand with its soft mouth. It wasn't looking for a treat, just sniffing tenderly before stepping up even closer and blowing some warm air into the girl's face. Instinctively, Eleanor gently blew back and it made a low greeting sound in its throat.

Just then, Isabel heaved herself up from the bench, startling it and it turned to canter off, disappearing down into a part of the field Eleanor could not see from where she was.

"Oh mum, you spooked it!" she exclaimed disappointedly and looked at her hand, "That was amazing."

"Spooked what?" Isabel frowned as she approached.

"Did you not see it?"

"See what?"

"The pony."

Chapter 4

For the rest of the day Eleanor felt out of synch - like a person on screen when the sound lags behind the picture. And every time she shut her eyes, there it was again.

The pony.

Looking at her with those eyes.

It had all been so surreal.

By supper time she wasn't even sure anymore whether it had been real or a ghost and found herself repeatedly rubbing the palm of her hand where it had sniffed her; or blowing against it to feel her breath ricocheting back into her face, in a desperate attempt to recreate *that* moment. Her mum seemed oblivious to Eleanor's state *(although one could never be sure with that woman)* and went to bed early, leaving Eleanor to pace the house, not knowing what to do with herself or where to settle. When, after some hours of touring between television, computer, bookshelf and fridge, Eleanor finally found her bed the restlessness morphed into a fitful sleep, spiked with what the Dutch called spaghetti dreams, from which she woke every half hour.

Peace, and with it some deeper sleep, finally came with a decision made just before dawn, on the way back from the toilet. She would get up early, before her mum, and go back there.

When she did find herself gently pulling the front door shut sometime in the paper round hours of the following morning that same peace turned into a continuously thumping heart as she felt the adrenaline pumping through her body. For a moment, she wanted to turn, go back into the house and scurry back to bed. But the idea of carrying on another day as restlessly as the night before seemed infinitely worse than the sheer fear of leaving a house she hardly called home to cycle around a forlorn part of a place she hardly knew and get lost on a twitten that potentially had wolves on it.

As she wheeled the bike out onto the empty road she was giving herself a well rehearsed lecture in the back of her mind on empty paths, rapists and strangers, while half visualising a funeral with herself in the starring role and her mum having an emergency Caesarian induced by the stress of burying her daughter.

Another, much more plausible, vision came to the front, showing her mum in bed right now, going into labour, calling for her with no reply.

She took a deep breath and pushed down on the pedals. She promised herself she would be quick and when she felt the cool air stream around her face it blew away all anxiety.

Without the walrus in tow and with the advantage of knowing the way now *(why was it that once you had gone a route before it always seemed shorter than the first time?)* it took her barely five minutes before she came to a halt in front of the entrance to the twitten. She could have cycled up to the metal gate but she thought it might frighten the pony *(if it was even there)* so she got off, locked the bike to the 'Private' fence and started walking. The path seemed darker than the day before but also, today, it seemed like just a path. There was nothing of note hanging in the air, no vibe to pick up on. She was almost sure the pony wouldn't be there but she trudged on, fighting pre-emptive disappointment by concentrating on her body.

Exertion from the ride, lack of sleep, anticipation and fear had drained her mouth of all moisture and she swallowed hard a couple of times, trying to generate some saliva with little success. By the time she came to the metal gate, she felt entirely consumed by a need for water.

One look across told her she had been right. No pony. She was about to turn back when she saw a tap on a post next to a water trough, where the pony *(or ghost of a pony)* had been standing the day before.

She hesitated but the thirst won. Heart beating wildly, she climbed over the gate and within seconds found herself holding her head sideways under a cool stream of water, drinking in large gulps. Lost in the sensation of satisfying a burning need, she didn't hear the thundering hooves until she turned off the tap, by which time they were so near it made her spin around.

There it was, only a few feet away, dust whirling around its legs where they had stopped dead in their tracks. It was facing her, head and tail held high, pumping air through flaring nostrils, making short little snorting noises and looking at her with utter indignation.

It was as beautiful as it was impressive and for a moment Eleanor thought her heart was going to explode with admiration. She could feel herself tremble as she took a deep breath and stretched out a hand in a pacifying gesture.

"Hey there," she said in a low voice, "I'm sorry, I didn't mean to intrude. I was seriously thirsty, you see. I wouldn't normally just come in uninvited. I'm not that kind of person. I just needed a little drink." She could see the pony's stance relax with every word and carried on talking without moving. "I cycled really hard to get here. I wanted to come see you. I'm not sure you remember me. I came yesterday. You sniffed my hand?" Eleanor knew that to an observer she would probably appear like the pony version of a mad cat lady in the making but the fact was, it was working. As she rambled on in a low voice, telling the pony about how she had thought about it all night and that she was new to the area and that she was going to start school in a few days, its head and tail lowered, indignation gave way to curiosity and it took a step forward.

Eleanor's heart, which had also quietened, made a leap again and she, too, took a step forward. The pony turned its head left then right, looking at her through each eye individually, gave another little snort and took another step forward. Eleanor gave it a second, then followed suit. She had stopped talking now and was waiting quietly for the pony to take another step. When it did, so did Eleanor. It felt a bit like a court dance out of some period drama. They were quite close now and Eleanor knew with the next step they would be within touching distance. She waited patiently for the pony to make another move. Suddenly something rustled in the bushes. Eleanor jumped out of her skin but the pony didn't seem bothered at all. It looked in the direction of the noise, making a low sound in its throat before its eyes and head seemed to trace something moving behind the hedgerow, down to the road. They came back to rest their gaze on Eleanor, almost mocking now, as if to say *you are a bit of a scaredy cat, aren't you?* ' - And then it just sauntered over to her as if the whole dance had been nothing but a game between old friends, gave her a gentle nudge in the rib cage with its nose and began lightly rubbing its forehead against Eleanor's shoulder. Eleanor was so surprised and overwhelmed by the sudden show of affection, she didn't think twice about what to do next. She started circling her fingernails behind the pony's ears, which it seemed to enjoy a lot, and then she moved around it, making the same circling motion down its neck and along its body. When she had finished with the left side, the pony turned to offer up its right and Eleanor gladly obliged.

By the time she had finished, her fingertips were coated in a funny grey film of skin particles and grease that smelled intensely of horse. It should have grossed her out but instead she smelled it with pride. It was proof that the pony wasn't a ghost. It was real and it let her touch it - and right now it was giving her another nudge, this time as if to say *'come with me'*.

It started moving towards the gate and when Eleanor didn't immediately follow, it stopped and turned its head to look at her. Eleanor started walking and side by side they reached the gate.

A row of carrot pieces had been left on the top bar and the pony picked them off one by one. When it had munched through all of them, it turned back to Eleanor and looked at her expectantly, its soft lips gently, carefully air-nibbling at Eleanor's shirt. Eleanor laughed.

"No, I'm sorry, I didn't bring you any food. I wouldn't just feed somebody else's pet. I wouldn't normally be in here either. Although I think I might come and visit you again tomorrow. – I had better stay on the other side though, I have an inkling you are 'private' property."

Though she was trying to sound joky and light-hearted, as she heard herself say it, she could feel tears welling up in her eyes. The idea of not having that same closeness again made her choke. She slung her arms around the pony's neck and gave it a hug. The pony seemed to echo her sadness and leant its head against her back, gently pushing her into its chest, returning the embrace. She let herself sink into it and for a moment felt engulfed with strength, love and wisdom in a way she never had before.

"Goodbye," Eleanor whispered, then let go, turned, climbed the gate without looking back and ran down the path.

By the time she got back to her bike she was sobbing violently, hardly able to see. She fumbled with the key for a good few minutes, dropped it, picked it up again - until somewhere in the periphery of her blurred vision she clocked a small, old fashioned dark green motorbike by the side of the road, black helmeted rider aboard, engine running but stationary as he fuffed with his gloves.

There was something familiar and reassuring in that small detail of his hands opening and closing to get the fingers sitting just right in the leather, reminding her of both Mick and Luke. She felt another pang of loss but this one came with Mick's no-nonsense voice of road training her for her cycling proficiency.

'Stop being ridiculous. This is not safe. You can't even see the road. Now pull yourself together, dry those tears, get on your bike and go.'

Home.

Sleep.

Tomorrow (today) is another day.

.Chapter 5

Eleanor was struggling with the smell and ambience of the best fish restaurant in town so shortly after getting up. Under normal circumstances she would have jumped for joy at her mum's announcement that Jon was coming to pick them up for dinner, taking them out to the world of baked Oysters served on silver platters atop white linen tables, followed by bream so fresh and perfectly cooked it practically still wriggled on the plate. Having slept the entire day away in dark, dreamless sleep, however, and only having been dragged back into consciousness roughly ten minutes before Jon's arrival, which in turn had only been about half an hour ago, she presently felt strongly like someone had changed channels on her life a bit too quickly.

She looked over at Jon and Isabel, talking animatedly about some musician or another's long awaited comeback. Her mum looked happy and relaxed in the company of one of her oldest friends and travel companions. *He never ages,* Eleanor thought to herself looking at Jon's bold head and bushy grey beard, *it's like he was born fifty.*

She let her eyes wander to the fourth chair at the table. It was still empty, soon to be filled by a new singing sensation on the folk circuit called Ebony Locks. Initially, Eleanor had thought it was a bit of a naff name until she had realised that it wasn't a band but a single singer-songwriter and that the name was genuine. The girl in question had just entered the restaurant and as the waiter showed her to the table, Eleanor's first, mildly cynical, thought revolved around wondering whether the 'sensation' part truly lay with the voice. Ebony was young *(nineteen? twenty?)*, impossibly tall and impossibly beautiful. Eleanor couldn't think of having met a single more aptly named person in her life. The high-cheekboned face, out of which gleamed big, friendly, dark eyes was framed in a mane of wild black locks that reached almost to the girl's waist. She was an absolute stunner. Yet there was also something enchantingly awkward about her, as she bent across the table nearly knocking over a glass in an attempt to stretch out a polite hand towards Isabel, appearing genuinely star struck.

"It's an absolute honour. I am so pleased to meet you. *Kittens in the Den* is one of my all time favourite pieces. When Jon said you might be able to play on my album, I thought he might be taking the Mick."

Scottish. Nice. Polite. I like. I wonder what mum makes of her.

"I'm recording for somebody's album?" Isabel asked, grinning at Jon in genuine amusement, "Wow. And when exactly am I doing this? Cause last time I checked, I was on a baby break and the last time I looked in the mirror, which if my memory serves me right, was about ten minutes ago, upstairs in this very establishment, the person looking back at me, hadn't even had said baby yet…"

"Tomorrow?" Jon grinned back.

"Ye what?" she looked back at Ebony, "Yes, you were right, he is definitely taking the piss."

Jon shrugged.

Ebony looked devastated but nodded her head as she finally sat down.

"I understand," she sighed, then looked at Jon, "We're just going to have to leave *Sea of Life* off, I guess. Signature track or not. Put something else on. There is no way I can afford to lose the time. And there is no way my folks can come up with more money for the studio once Ginny is better. And it's got to go out before Cambridge. I can't do Cambridge and not have anything to sell. That would be stupendously stupid."

Eleanor watched Isabel watching Ebony.

She knew that this could go either way for the girl sitting next to her now, looking down at the starched table cloth and nervously kneading the knuckles of a gorgeous pair of hands. From listening to the conversation earlier Eleanor knew that Ebony played the guitar. If unlucky, the classically trained violinist sitting across from her would sneer at the young talent's choice of instrument to drown out the disappointment in her own career with a healthy dose of arrogance. If lucky, the all time favourite session fiddle player of the European folk scene *(quote, unquote some fanzine or other)* would benevolently bestow wisdom upon the young musician at the beginning of her journey.

Isabel sighed.

Good sign.

"I tell you what, let's take it from the top, shall we? As you may have gathered, Mister here didn't mention any work commitments. If I remember correctly, the phone call went something like 'I have a day off recording and I would like to take you out for dinner to welcome you to my home town'. I should, of course, have known that there was some sort of ulterior motive at the point where he added 'and there is someone I would love you to meet'. Also, if there hadn't been an ulterior motive, it would have been fish and chips on the beach – not fancy pants posh flippers. Ah well. - I take it you put up the money for the studio time yourself?"

Ebony looked up, tired, deflated but with a flicker of hope and nodded. Eleanor felt sorry for her. There was a desertedness surrounding her that somehow reminded her of the pony.

Heaven help, I'm obsessed, how on earth do you get from here to there in two seconds flat?

She surreptitiously smelled her fingertips. Even after a number of hand washes and a shower she could still faintly smell the horse odour underneath, as if it had etched itself indelibly into her prints.

"My folks have. They really believe in me," Ebony answered.

"Do you believe in you?" Isabel coldly pursued it further. *Man, she can be such a bitch.*

Ebony shrugged.

"I like my stuff. I write it because I want to hear something that I can't hear unless I write it. Define 'belief in myself'. I believe I'm a halfway decent person, I believe I write good songs, I believe I make a fairly mean breakfast, but I have no idea whether I'll be successful. How could I?" Here the rehearsed part of the answer fizzled out and she swallowed hard before continuing. "You to me are a real case in point. You should have been famous. I mean really famous, not just a bit famous. I wasn't being polite, I really love *Kittens in the Den.* With a passion. I've listened to it at least once a week for the last ten years. I mean, it's brilliant. Properly, properly brilliant. It grows with you as you get older…"

She looked up, straight at Isabel. Eleanor could see a slight tremor above her top lip as she carried on.

"But you've never put out anything else. I've looked. I still look. Nothing," Ebony hesitated, "Why not?"

Isabel started laughing, the belly laugh that Eleanor loved so much. The one that was her mum's, not some random backstage persona's.

She'll do it. Whatever this girl needs, she's got it.

"Rock stars," her mum burst out, "Children and rock stars. Or rather childish rock stars and one very mature child. - Keep looking. One day I just might surprise you. Oh look, a waiter."

Eleanor didn't like her mum referring to the JML's in this derogatory way. She didn't like it when she portrayed them as useless and herself as this Übermutter who'd brought them all up. In between obsessing about the pony and feeling out of synch, Eleanor had gone back in her head again and again to the speech her mum had delivered the day before. It simply wasn't true. It hadn't all been about them. They had cared. They had nursed Eleanor when she'd had chickenpox and Isabel through her fatigues induced by too much work and not enough recognition. Without them, Eleanor wouldn't have been able to cook for herself, ride a bike, swim or do a handstand. She would never have seen Star Wars 4, 5 and 6 *first* or read Northern Lights. She wouldn't have known the difference between a two stroke and a four stroke engine or how to tell a bean stalk from a cannabis plant *(maybe not the best example)* or…. The point was, they were all decent people and in their different ways, she loved them all and they had all loved her. She hoped they still did, although other than Jerry they all seemed to have faded away, busy with new women and new other fathers' children.

Her thoughts went back to the morning, to the man on the little green bike, wriggling his hands in the gloves and a wave of love washed over her. For Jerry, Mick and Luke - but also for this stranger, for being there to remind her, just when she had needed reminding.

Lost in this funny sea of love and loss, she had missed a large chunk of the exchange with the young, pimply, gel-haired waiter whose blatant lust for Ebony resulted in some awkward fidgeting as he took their orders. She picked up just as he was eyeing her up with unhidden disdain.

"…and I'm sorry but at Oyster's we do not carry a child's menu, I'm afraid. I could, of course, ask the chef to prepare something for the little lady…"

It was then that Eleanor realised that until now she had kept herself out of the room to the point where nobody had bothered to introduce her to Ebony or acknowledged her presence in any way.

Not even Eleanor herself.

She sat up and jolted herself into the scenario. Suddenly visible, she locked eyes with him.

"I don't believe anyone asked for a child's menu."

She let her eyes wander down to the white towel that served as an apron in front of his crotch, then back up to his eyes again, from there she glanced sideways at Ebony and then back into his eyes, raising an eyebrow in the process.

"Bring me half a dozen oysters. Three raw, three baked. Then the pan-fried bream, thank you very much."

He seemed rooted to the spot, embarrassed into immobility as he blushed bright red.

Suddenly Eleanor felt a little sorry for him. After all he wasn't the first to make that mistake and would probably not be the last.

She added in a more friendly tone, "Off you hop," and as if released from a spell he turned and left.

Ebony gasped, watched him disappear then turned to Eleanor wide-eyed, suddenly looking distinctly younger and even less reassured than before.

"That was fantastic. How? What an arse. Can you teach me to do that?"

Eleanor grinned.

"I think it only works if you are 4 foot 3 and a sprite, not if you are 6 foot and a goddess. If you did it, they might take it as an invitation. - Hi, I'm Eleanor."

"I'm Ebony."

"So I've gathered. Pleased to meet you."

Chapter 6

Being alone in the house for the first time since they'd
moved here felt strange but also somehow long overdue.
There had been a brief exchange between Isabel and her,
bleary eyed, at circa 7am, about whether Eleanor was
allowed to stay behind or whether – as had naturally been
assumed – she would accompany her mother to the
recording studio and sit around all day twiddling her
thumbs, as on countless occasions before. Once, Eleanor
had spent an entire summer in a cellar in Amsterdam,
listening to a Belgian combo recording modernised
medievil *(spelling intended)* French folk music.
When a gentle reminder of this hadn't served as a get out
of studio free card this morning, Eleanor had played her
trump by threatening to call Kjell and tell on her mum if
she was made to go. In the end, an angry Isabel had
thrown her hands up in the air and had left her to it with
strict instructions not to leave the house unless it was on
fire.
At first, just after the front door had been pulled shut with
more of a noise than was strictly necessary, Eleanor had
felt guilty for having given her mum a hard time but now
she was enjoying the first real chance to say hello to her
new home.
It was hot outside again and Eleanor relished walking
around the house just wrapped in a towel with her wet hair
dripping down her exposed neck and shoulder blades,
where the drops would be cooled from the breeze she'd
created by opening every single window she came past.
She had noticed the odour in the house slowly change
during Kjell's absence, the whiff of dentist having been
almost entirely expunged by her mum's smell and that of
her own. As she went in and out of every single room of
the house, remaining just one step inside the door of those
that weren't communal - such as Kjell's study

(surprisingly dark and snuggly) or the chaos room that was to be her mum's den *(not that one could have got further than putting one foot in)* or even the baby's future kingdom - yet thoroughly inspecting all others, she slowly realised that despite being bare and still somewhat nondescript and terribly tidy in most places, it was a good house. She was starting to understand why her mum felt she could be creative here. *(Why on earth was it, that you often only really got the people closest to you after you'd had a massive row?)*

While many *(and there had been many)* of their previous pads had been cosy, cluttered, colourful and chaotic they had also often felt somewhat tired. A bit like a parent after a children's birthday party: benevolent and happy but utterly exhausted and begging you to calm down and give it a rest.

This one, on the other hand, felt fresh and friendly, ready for adventure. She finished her round and returned to the kitchen, the only room beside her own she already had an ongoing relationship with, got some cereal and took it upstairs.

Getting to the top of the landing she saw that she'd left Kjell's study door wide open and went to shut it, stopping again in amazement in the door frame. It was so utterly unlike the Kjell she had experienced so far, so unlike the bright, light, blank creaminess of the rest of the house, it was almost as if this room was an impostor. Her curiosity suddenly winning over her natural respect for personal space, Eleanor found herself setting down the cereal bowl on the floor and instead of closing the door from the outside, she went in and shut it from inside, heart pounding deep in her chest.

Ridiculous, it's not as if I'm going to steal anything or read his diary.

She stood in the middle of the room and looked around.

All four walls were covered floor to ceiling in oak bookshelves, ram packed with books, from antiquarian leather tomes to modern paperbacks, absorbing most of the light that came from the single window and turning the sunshine falling in right now into a dark orange like the last embers of a dying fire. There was no desk, just a couple of heavy but comfy looking antique armchairs and a coffee table with a phone by the window. It was tidy but cosy and, she realised with a jolt, did not remotely smell of dentist.

It smelled of books.

No kidding, she thought sarcastically to herself as she started slowly walking along the rows, deciphering the titles. Or some of the titles, for Kjell evidently did not just speak Swedish and English but appeared to be able to read German, French and Latin as well. She hadn't known that. *If I'm honest, I don't really know anything about him at all.*

She was trying to find a discernible pattern in the order of the books that seemed to cover every subject known to man and every period of literature from Chaucer to Pullman but conceded that where content and language was concerned they had been put in at random, purely according to size. Having finished going along the top rows, she was bending down now to look at the floor level, where graphic novels *(really ?!?)*, comics *(seriously ?!?)* and coffee table books fought for space with a Britannica and some Swedish encyclopaedia of similar dimensions. She let her eyes wander along the spines when suddenly her heart made a leap.

Häst the title on the dust jacket read and above it was the tiny picture of a horse's head looking dreamily into the camera, mane flowing in the breeze. Eleanor's heart began beating wildly again as she put her hand out to pull the book off the shelf.

Just in that moment, the phone rang and made her jump out of her skin. Her pulse pounding in her ears, shock tears welling up in her eyes, she went to answer it.

"Hello?"

"Eleanor?"

It was Kjell.

Guiltily she looked at the book in her hand.

"Everything alright there?"

"Yup. All good."

The front showed the same photograph in a bigger frame. The horse was standing on a hill top, mane flowing in the wind with a blonde, Viking-eyed boy of about ten in distinctly 70s clothing sitting astride it, bareback and bridleless, hugging its neck and smiling into the camera.

"Can you put Isabel on, please?"

Eleanor swallowed.

"She isn't here."

"What do you mean she isn't there?" there was mild panic in his voice, "Where is she? And why aren't you with her?"

"Don't worry, all good, nothing's happened, she is with Jon."

"Jon who?"

"Simmons."

"What? The guy with the studio?"

"Uhu."

There was a pause, something that sounded like swearing and a sigh.

"I knew I shouldn't have left. She is working, isn't she?"

"Just today. Maybe part of tomorrow. Depends. – Don't worry, Jon will take good care of her. First sign of anything, he'll take her to hospital. He *loves* mum. They've been best friends for, like, ever."

"I'm going to ring her on her mobile then."

"It'll be switched off. And even if it isn't, I wouldn't if I was you. You'll just piss her off. She doesn't do being told what to do."

"Yes," he sighed, "I know. - That's why I'm with her. - Thank you Eleanor."

"What for?"

"Being straight with me."

"You make it easy."

There was a pause as Eleanor was waiting for him to say goodbye and ring off but he didn't. Suddenly she remembered where he was and what he was doing there.

"Kjell?" She asked, staring at the photograph's much younger version of him.

"Yes?"

"Are *you* alright?"

His exhaustion was nearly tangible through the phone.

"Not really, no. It's… I just wanted to hear her voice."

"She'll be back tonight. I told her if she came back later than eight, I'd ring you and rat on her."

He snorted a laugh.

"Thank you Eleanor. - I haven't had the chance to tell you this but I'm really glad you came with the package. You take care of yourself. - I've got to go back in. - Later."

"Later," Eleanor echoed and they put down the phones in unison.

She stared at the receiver for a while longer then took a closer look at the book, which she had rested on the coffee table.

She opened it gently.

It appeared to be a photo manual on caring, grooming and riding horses, showing the same boy and horse in all illustrations. There was a warm, true quality to the pictures. You could tell they had not been staged but had been taken over the course of a year as and when things were happening and that this had been a real boy with his real horse.

Looking at the pictures she could feel the restlessness starting to gnaw at her soul again and after a few minutes she shut it unceremoniously, put it back in its place, left the study and went to get ready.

Chapter 7

When she got to the gate the pony was already there, head hanging over the top bar, dozing in the shade to avoid the midday heat. Today Eleanor had decided to cycle all the way up and the pony opened one lazy eye as it heard the clicking of the spokes but didn't take any more notice of the bike's - or Eleanor's - arrival. Once it had determined the nature of the intrusion, it went straight back to dozing, occasionally shaking its head lightly to get rid of the flies accumulating on its face. Eleanor stopped, slightly disappointed at the lack of enthusiasm on the animal's part but also understanding of the creature's need to rest.

Today, it looked old and a bit tired.

Eleanor wheeled her bike to behind the bench, sat down quietly and watched it dream. Its bottom lip was flopping down and gave the impression of total relaxation but the ears kept twitching and from time to time a shiver rippled through the whole body. Eleanor wondered how one could be so caught in reverie yet so alert at the same time.

She knew it knew she was there.

They remained like this for a while.

After about twenty minutes, Eleanor's bum started getting numb from sitting on the cold bench and she began wondering what on earth she was doing here.

She got up and turned back to her bicycle. There was a drawn out snort behind her back, followed by a low throaty noise. She turned back and saw it looking at her with alert, amused eyes, repeating the low throaty noise. Eleanor couldn't help but beam at it. She walked over to rub its face with her flat palm and slung her arms around its neck. She inhaled deeply to take in its smell with every fibre of her being. She let go and just like the previous day it rubbed her back gently against the shoulder then made another throaty noise before turning away from the gate and walking towards the tree line. When Eleanor didn't follow it stopped and looked around at her.

She climbed up onto the gate and called loudly: "I'm sorry, I really don't think I'm allowed in there. You come back here."

"I wouldn't worry about that if I was you. Owner is as good as dead. Hardly gonna shoot you. Go ahead, she wants to play with you," came a muffled voice, passing by behind her.

Eleanor spun around on the gate and saw the back of the biker as he was slowly pushing the green motorbike laden with shopping up the path. Catching a closer glimpse of the machine this time, she could see it was a little Yamaha, maybe 50cc, with a distinct vintage look about it – real old school as Mike would have said.

"Are you sure?" she shouted after him.

He didn't turn or change pace but briefly raised a gloved hand above his head with a thumb's up before quickly taking it down to steady the bike again. A little further up, he disappeared through a hole in the wall.

She hesitated a moment then jumped over into the paddock. The pony had vanished into the tree line and Eleanor couldn't see her *(she, he'd said – it was a mare)* anymore.

Suddenly a football came flying out of the trees and landed directly in front of Eleanor's feet. Eleanor frowned at it, looking around, unsure as to who might have kicked it. A second later, the pony trotted out from behind a tree, head lowered, eyes on the ball. It stopped some distance away, looked up at Eleanor, then back at the ball, muscles tense, waiting like a cat waits for the string to be moved. Eleanor gave the football a gentle kick and it rolled slowly towards the mare. The pony ran at it, stopped abruptly and rolled it gently back to the girl with her nose. Eleanor laughed and kicked it back, a bit more forcefully this time, slightly to the left of the mare. The pony watched it go past, arched her back and kicked out *(is that what they call a buck?)* in exuberance, charged after the ball, rounded it up and kicked it back towards Eleanor.

Oh my word, I'm playing football with a pony, was the last clear thought the girl managed before she let herself be engulfed by the game, which became faster and more hilarious with every minute, soon stretching over the entire field.

Half an hour or so later they were back by the tap, panting, pouring with sweat, exhausted and happy. After they had both had a long drink, the mare from the trough and Eleanor from the tap, the girl held her head under the stream of water to cool down. The pony, who'd quenched its main thirst but was still lazily sucking up little gulps of water and had kept one eye on her companion, suddenly dipped her nose right into the trough and began splashing the water around until Eleanor was drenched head to foot. Eleanor squealed, then laughed and started splashing the mare back. Once they were both dripping they stopped and moved back into the sunshine in the field. The little mare put her head down and began grazing, rhythmically ripping at the grass with her teeth. Eleanor leant against her, feeling the warm water on the pony's coat, getting herself even wetter *(if that was still possible)* than before. She stuck her nose deep into the hair and took in this new aroma of wet horse until she could feel the muscles tense under her face. A ripple went through the pony and she stepped back from it in time to get caught in a shower of drops glistening in the sun as the mare shook the water off.

"I wish I could do that," Eleanor stated and as the pony stopped to move off, she took her shirt off *(not much to see yet anyway and if anyone is watching: it's basically a triple A cup - now you know)* and wrung it out best as she could. The animal meanwhile had started pawing the ground and let herself flop down for a roll in the dirt. A gentle breeze had gathered around them and while the pony was having a field day rolling this way and that, all four legs sticking up in the air in between as she rubbed her back into the ground, Eleanor stretched her arms up above her head, letting the wind flow over her naked torso.

For a moment, she felt totally free.

Then a different feeling crept along her spine. Someone *was* watching. She was being watched, *had been watched* all along. And not by an animal.

Shit, shit, shit.

She hurried over to the mare who was back on her feet now and hid close to her while trying to get the clammy shirt back on her body.

Eleanor realised that she was trapped.

As long as she stayed close to the pony and they stayed on open ground she was safe. But eventually she would have to get back to her bike and onto the dark path. What, if whoever was watching her *(she could feel the eyes still on her),* was waiting for her? What could she do?

I should ring mum, ring the studio, tell them where I am. Get them to come and get me. Forget getting into trouble for leaving the house. Just get them to come.

She fished her mobile out of her dripping shorts pocket. It was dead, soaked into oblivion. Eleanor stared at it. She was on her own.

'Not that a mobile telephone is actually company, or a safety device for that matter,' she heard her grandmother rant in her head.

Panic slowly rising, she realised that she could either run or saunter *(alert, so as to run when necessary).* She decided for the latter. She gave the obliviously munching pony a quick hug and whispered, "Wish me luck," in its ear, then set off slowly, pretending to push a couple of buttons on her phone and putting it to her ear.

"Hi mum," she said loudly into nothingness, "yes I'm just leaving here now. Be back home in ten. If not, send out the cavalry. Yes, mum?"

The pretend voice on the other end of the line went into a long monologue about something, punctuated by affirmative noises on Eleanor's part as she looked over the gate, up and down the path *(nothing apparent – but oh so many hiding places)*, then climbed over one-handed. Once on the other side, Eleanor got her keys out, selected the longest and sharpest and put it between middle and ring finger to stick out of her fist, clenched around the remaining keys. Thus armed she went over to her bike, having picked up her part of the imaginary conversation again with a long list of suggestions as to what they could eat for dinner *(she was starving)*. She knew that once she'd reached the bike there would be a moment of defenselessness while she unlocked it, for which she would have to unclench her fist, hang up the phone and bend down. Before she did, she briefly closed her eyes and felt around the ether. The watching had stopped.

There was some kind of residue but she wasn't under the microscope any longer.

Good.

She took a deep breath and calmly, *slowly* finished the act, before getting on her bike and tearing down the path as fast as she could.

Chapter 8

Even if fear had not kept her from going back the next day
- which it might well have done despite finding the small
can of pepper spray Jerry had given her for her 10th
birthday, while unpacking the last of her removal boxes -
there simply hadn't been an opportunity to slip out of the
house. Not even at dawn.

Isabel had brought back half the studio the night before,
having successfully helped to wrap Ebony's album for
her. They had sat up till sunrise and filled the house with
that familiar spirit of a bunch of high on music recording
artists.

Isabel had been radiant, sailing through the people like a
huge ship, proffering cups of tea and single malt Whiskeys
for those not entirely on the wagon, alongside a variety of
cheeses.

Over the smoker's corner in the garden hung the familiar
scent of mellow weed, a smell Eleanor loved although she
wasn't overly keen on stoners who seemed to waffle about
life a lot without actually living it much and who would
eat all the sweets in the house. Nevertheless, Eleanor liked
this crowd, liked the folk scene musicians, none of whom
took themselves too seriously, better than the crowd that
surrounded her father: The rock stars with the powdered
mirrors, bourbons, beer and bimbos and the over-inflated
cocaine fuelled egos or – even worse – the self pitying
junkie whine, hell-bent on proving that just because
something was a cliché, it didn't mean it wasn't true or
that they weren't going to live up to it.

She had enjoyed the party's company and had tried hiding
in it from the recurring feeling of unease that kept
creeping into her consciousness every time she let her
thoughts wander back to the pony.

After the event, when she had got back home, she'd let
herself realise how much danger she had potentially put

herself in and it was making her feel mildly violated but also simply angry.

It had been such fun, she'd felt so free. Why couldn't life be that simple? Why was there always something lurking in the shadows? Why did she have to be born a scrawny little girl and not a burly bully boy who could just run freely, without fear? Or at least a bit taller, a bit more physically imposing – a bit like the beautiful Scottish girl all of this was in aid of.

She was still reeling with these thoughts the next morning, which strictly speaking happened around midday, when she was entering the living room carrying a tray with marmite toast and tea for Ebony who'd crashed on the sofa. Ebony was already awake, sitting up with her back against the armrest, looking at her as she entered.

"You're an angel, Eleanor. I could have got it myself, you know."

Eleanor put the tray down on the coffee table and muttered, "No problem."

Ebony cocked her head at the younger girl and smiled. "An angry angel."

"Hm," Eleanor handed Ebony the cup absentmindedly.

"Thank you. - Are you okay? Am I in your space?"

"What?" Eleanor looked up, "Don't be silly. - No, I just got stuff on my mind."

Ebony laughed and gestured for Eleanor to sit down next to her.

"I get that. Care to elaborate?"

I don't even know you, Eleanor thought but sat down on the edge of the sofa anyway. Everything else seemed rude. They sat in silence.

"Hey," Ebony suddenly said softly before leaning over and scooping her up in a hug. Until her face got swamped in Ebony's long wild curls, Eleanor hadn't realised that silent tears had been running down her cheeks. She

38

stiffened, retracted, snuffled loudly and wiped the tears away with the long sleeve of her pyjama top.

"I'm fine. Just angry. I cry when I'm angry."

"Sorry, I didn't mean to...." Ebony fumbled awkwardly for words then gave up, before crinkling up her nose and sniffing the air, "You smell of horse."

"I doubt it," Eleanor's reply came quickly. *(Why is it such a secret? Why do I not want anyone to know? It's stupid.)* "Must be a hallucination then. - I guess I miss my girl so much, I can smell her all the way from Scotland," Ebony smiled mischievously, "or, you're not a sprite as you would have it but a kelpie - you're much too beautiful to be a sprite anyway."

"Yeah right," Eleanor snorted, then added after a pause, "What on earth is a kelpie?"

"A water spirit in the shape of a horse. - It's my mare's name."

"You have a horse?" Eleanor looked up in surprise. *Why was it, that once you were interested in something it would suddenly pop up everywhere, when beforehand it hadn't been anywhere around you at all, ever? Bizarre.* "Actually, she's a pony. A Dales – 14.1 on her tippy toes. We look a bit ridiculous these days but who cares. I love her to bits. I've had her since I was seven. She was my first, second *and* third pony. People keep telling me to get something bigger, that I've outgrown her, but we're alright. I have to be careful that our legs don't get tangled in a canter but hey," Ebony shrugged, eyes gleaming with love and enthusiasm, "my competition days are over anyway, I've got to concentrate on the music if I want to make a living from it one day. The Queen rides a Dales, you know. And what's good for your queen is good enough for me. Admittedly, she's 5 foot nothing and I'm bloody 5 foot 11 and a half but we wouldn't be able to afford another and no way is my Kelpie going to some brat who happens to not be doomed with an overactive growth gland. Here," while she had been talking, Ebony had picked up her bag from next to the sofa, had extracted a phone and was presently shoving the display under Eleanor's nose. It showed the older girl sitting on a completely black, sturdy and very hairy pony with a chunky but elegant head, her long legs dangling a good foot or so beyond the belly line. Nevertheless, there was nothing awkward about the picture. Girl and pony looked like a team of odd socks but like a team nevertheless. Suddenly Eleanor burst into laughter. Ebony retracted the phone, hurt in her eyes.

"It's not *that* funny," she mumbled defensively, suddenly looking very young again.

"No!" Eleanor exclaimed, and grabbed the older girl by the shoulders, "It's not that. You two look lovely together. I was just..." she needed to rein in the laughter before she could carry on, "It's just so ridiculous. There is me all angry cause I'm fed up with being so bloody tiny and scrawny, thinking I would give my eye teeth for some of what you've got and there is you, grumbling cause you're so tall. Isn't it stupid?"

Ebony smiled shyly.

"So it's not the picture?"

"Are you insane? You look great. She looks great. Let's have another look."

Ebony handed the phone back.

Very pretty. But not as pretty as my one. – My one? Oh dear, I need to snap out of this.

"She is very pretty."

"Very old blood line, I'll have you know. There are a few people interested in her. But no. She's mine. Mine, mine, mine. And nothing and nobody is going to come between us," Ebony laughed as she took the phone back, dropped it in her bag and made to get up, "Which is also why I'd better be getting my arse out of here and to the airport.

With a bit of luck, if there are no delays, I'll still have time for a mini hack tonight."

I hate you, Eleanor thought with much love in her heart, *but you're right: nothing and nobody.*

Afterwards the resolve had been there but every second of her day had been spent in the company of an overtired but elated Isabel. There was tidying the house *('Which one of these bloody stoners left a cereal bowl on the landing!'),* shopping for a new phone *('How on earth can you possibly drop a phone in the bath tub?!?')* and for a jumper in the new school colour *('We'll get you a proper uniform tomorrow before school.'* – Eleanor had her doubts that they would have one her size.) And last but not least, Kjell returning.

Eleanor watched from the top of the landing as he walked through the door late that evening, took his shoes off and fell into his pregnant woman's arms like a drowning man who'd reached land. He looked exhausted and pale but happy to be home. When he had kissed Isabel gently on mouth, eyes and forehead, he looked up the stairs at Eleanor, a twinkle in his grey-green eyes.

"Hi Eleanor, how was the quiet girlie weekend?"

Something had shifted.

Chapter 9

By 3 o'clock Monday she felt totally knackered. So many faces, so many names, so many *dynamics*. She had been in this situation before, a few times, but the tone was markedly different this time around.

Changing schools at infant and junior level had been frightening but also fun. The children had always been friendly, curious and excited about her arrival, wherever she'd turned up. There had been the odd stab at her size but generally the teachers had, without fail, bent over backwards to make her feel welcome and done everything in their power, which at that level seemed infinite, to integrate her as quickly as possible. She'd swiftly made the transition from curio to valued, if somewhat quiet and often invisible, resident pixie.

Changing at lower senior level was a whole different ball game.

She had expected as much but she hadn't counted on how exhausting being regarded as yet another chore on an already overflowing plate (teachers) and potential threat to final, painfully over the last two years negotiated, group dynamics (fellow students) would be.

There hadn't been a single welcoming face or friendly gesture from anyone all day.

No nastiness either, just total indifference.

At first she'd found it a relief, not having to smile and talk and answer questions all day, allowing her to melt into the background and figure out a pretext on which she could leave the house later and visit the pony but by now she felt tired, vulnerable and very, very lonely.

She missed the little mare terribly.

She had set her alarm for five o'clock, planning to sneak out and get back before Kjell got up at six thirty but then she had lain awake until way past midnight and had slept right through it - dreaming she was getting up, dreaming she got ready, dreaming she sneaked out of the house, dreaming the feel of the pony's soft mouth nuzzling against her palm. Until a loud knock on the bedroom door had dragged her from that reality into this one.

In the end, she'd had to finish breakfast in the car while berating her mum for not letting her go on the bus or by bike on her own. Although part of her had felt happy that her mum had insisted on being there for her on her first day, a larger part had worried every time she had looked over at her mum's gigantic bump practically touching the steering wheel as they were driving along. It didn't need much to figure out that even a comparatively minor accident at this stage could kill the baby. And she had used that observation shamelessly to negotiate coming home alone on the bus. Her mum had reluctantly agreed, still worried about it being a new town and various other what-ifs and if-whens until Eleanor had erupted in a long monologue, stating that after three weeks new wasn't shiny anymore; that it was five stops and fairly obvious in which direction she had to go; that she had to start doing it on her own sooner or later because like it or lump it the baby was coming; and that she wasn't ever going to find out any what-ifs and if-whens if she wasn't allowed to go and do anything at all – by which point her mum had been reduced to ball of hysterical laughter and had declared defeat.

It had been the best moment of the day so far and Eleanor was clinging to the memory like a life raft as she was slowly crossing the car park to get to the bus stop.

She could see that there were still throngs of people waiting and stopped to get her phone out, intending to send her mum a quick message, saying that she was going to hang around for the next, emptier bus. The last thing she fancied right now was being caught in the middle of inane chatter, engulfed in other people's body odour masked with bad deodorant choices.

"So, what's your face, what's your story then? You some kind of genius or something?"

Eleanor looked up from her phone to find herself being eyed up by a comparatively tall, good looking strawberry blonde with a fully fledged cleavage squished into the tailored white blouse that was one of two choices within the uniform regulations of the establishment (quote, unquote the lady with the piercings in the office who had given her the low-down on appropriate attire rules after conceding that a proper uniform for Eleanor would have to be tailor made).

The girl was in Eleanor's year and they'd shared some lessons today, although Eleanor wasn't entirely sure, which ones. She'd vaguely registered her as quite mouthy, flirtatious with the teachers and immensely self assured with no evidence of either intelligence or idiocy as yet.

"Come again?" Eleanor replied quietly, holding her gaze - something the girl obviously hadn't expected. The girl's voice rose a fraction.

"Well, if you're in my year you must be extremely clever, right? Either that - or a midget. So which one is it, genius or midget?"

"The verdict's still out on that," Eleanor replied.

Weird, normally this shit only happens if they have a crowd to play to or if they are seriously thick. She doesn't sound thick and there isn't a crowd – who is she performing to?

No sooner had the thought formed when she could suddenly feel a presence stepping up right behind her, so strong, so powerful, it was almost sickening and she wondered how she could possibly not have noticed it come closer before.

Shit, she thought, *shit, shit, shit – this is it, the scenario they warn you about. They got me. I'm about to be...what?*

Then it hit her: she hadn't noticed it before because *it had been there for days.*

Subdued, ticking away in the background, *since...since when exactly?*

Oddly, there was reassurance in that.

"Piss off Tinkerbelle," said a softly dark, menacing voice over her head, "she's mine to pick a bone with. Get out of her face."

Just before she turned on her heels and hurried off, there was a flicker of pain in the girl's eyes as she looked up at the carrier of the voice that would have made Eleanor feel almost sorry for her, had it not been for the rising anger over the realisation that she had just been used as some kind of haggling object between two people who obviously had issues with one another.

Great, she thought, *just what I needed. Huzar.*

She wanted to start walking but somehow felt rooted to the spot. She raised her head, still not turning to look at this presence, this *person.*

Instead, she kept staring after the girl as she vanished into the distance and at the emptying bus stop ahead.

"Tinkerbelle?" she heard herself say, sounding quite assured, amused even, "Is that for real?"

He stepped up from behind to level with her side by side. She still didn't look at him but felt the warmth emanating from him as they stood shoulder to shoulder.

Well, nipple to top of head, really.

The quality of the air had changed, rather than overwhelmed and nauseous, she felt safe now.

Safer than she had all day.

"Yep," he said, "it's for real. Sister's called Wendy and all."

"Poor thing."

"Quite."

She didn't want to leave this moment but knew it was over, neither did she feel ready to look into his face. She started walking. He kept pace.

"What's your name?"

"Eleanor."

"I'm Peter."

"You part of their family then?"

"Funny. - Don't even go there. - Actually, most people call me Pike."

"Like the fish."

He laughed quietly.

"Guess so."

They'd arrived at the now deserted bus stop just as a bus pulled up. The doors opened. Eleanor made towards the steps. Pike put one hand lightly on her shoulder and with the other waved the bus driver off, who promptly shut the doors and pulled away again. Eleanor could feel her heart beating in her throat.

"What the…"

He didn't let her finish.

"Look at me."

She turned towards him but remained staring at his midriff, still avoiding his face.

Suddenly, she was scared again. She wasn't quite sure, what of exactly. It was very unlikely he was going to rape or murder her, here, in the bus stop opposite the main entrance to the school. Besides, he didn't *feel* like that. He felt…disappointed.

In her.

Specifically.

Not in a generic way.

And she had an inkling that it was a just and righteous disappointment and that she was about to end up feeling mortified.

But how? She had never met him until about three minutes ago.

Her thoughts were still reeling when he said it again, very softly but with the same authority with which he had waved the bus driver off.

"Eleanor, look at me."

She did.

She didn't know what she had expected but what she saw somehow didn't fit it at all, yet at the same time was the only logical conclusion to that voice. *The only face possible.*

It was a broad, kind face, covered in freckles that were almost invisible against his dark reddish skin tone and which were on the left side partially connected *(join the dots)* by a few dozen lighter coloured old scars, as if he had once upon a time fallen through a glass door or skidded on gravel. His wide-bridged nose had clearly been broken at least once and remained slightly crooked. His hair was blackish brown and unruly, sticking out in all directions as thick spikes, not in a teased and pruned style but in a self cut, I-don't-give-a fashion. His smile revealed a chipped upper incisor on the right and reached all the way to his eyes, which she was still avoiding.

"I'm not gonna eat you. Actually look at me."

When she did, she realised immediately why she hadn't wanted to. They were amber, the colour of liquid honey or, more precisely, like a cat's who'd missed out on the green gene, which was disconcerting enough but, more importantly, they *burned*. With all the emotions under the sun: anger and hope, pain and pleasure, bliss and despair – and right now with utter disapproval.

They reached right into her soul, making her feel totally naked.

Under a microscope.

His voice betrayed the eyes and remained measured, friendly even.

"I said I had a bone to pick with you and that's exactly what I'm going to do. I'll make it brief, so you can catch the next bus. Here goes: unless you're ill or it is a proper emergency, you cannot ever not turn up. Capiche? If you are gonna be patchy, don't bother at all."

He let it hang for a moment, broke eye contact, sighed and sounded resigned when he carried on.

"The Mouse waited for you by the gate all day yesterday. It's bad enough playing with a happy horse's heart but she's very low right now. She lost the last of her companions a month ago and she's lonely. – So, bottom line, either you come *every* day, summer or winter, rain or shine, or, " he briefly leant forward to level with her eyes, looking straight into her core again, "you fuck off out of our lives completely. Your choice. - There's your bus." With that he turned away and walked to the car park without looking back, leaving Eleanor shaking and with her heart beating not just in her throat but all the way up to behind the ears. She stumbled onto the bus and into a chair.

As she sat down she caught a last glimpse of him in the car park, unlocking his motorbike.

Chapter 10

"Excellent, I'm glad you're back," Isabel was standing in the doorway ready to leave when Eleanor returned, "Kjell is going to pick me up any minute now. We have a midwife appointment in half an hour. How was it? Did you make any friends?"

I'm not seven, mum! I don't make friends in a day anymore.

But she grasped the opportunity.

"Actually yes, I did. They've asked me over to their house this afternoon. They live over by that twitten we took the bike ride to. Is that alright?"

Lying never sat well with Eleanor and it surprised her how smoothly this one had come over her lips.

Kjell had pulled up to the curb.

"That's fantastic!" Isabel beamed, "Of course you can. Shall we drop you off?"

"Nah," Eleanor replied, "I want to get changed first and it's not really your direction, is it? I'll bike it. It's only down the road."

Kjell had got out of the car, gone to the passenger side to open the door for Isabel and was gesturing at her to get moving.

"Excellent," Isabel, who had started waddling towards Kjell, carried on over her shoulder, "Right. Dinner is at eight. Don't be late. And enjoy!"

That was the strange thing about Isabel: one minute Eleanor had to fight for every inch of freedom, the next she'd treat her like an adult and just let her get on with it. The tricky thing was to know, which minute was which.

That was easy.

Isabel stopped at the car door, looking back over at Eleanor.

"Oh. What's the girl's name?"

Errr...

"I don't actually know her real name? Everyone calls her Mouse."

Isabel frowned.

"Oh, well, have fun. Later."

Isabel rolled herself into the car and Kjell shut the door. He quickly waved at Eleanor then jumped into the driver's seat and off they went.

When Eleanor got to the gate, the pony was nowhere to be seen. The girl looked at her hands against the metal of the top bar, felt her body poised for climbing over, then changed her mind.

She knew what she had to do first.

She sighed, let go, turned and carried on up the path. After about twenty yards she spotted the high garden gate through which he had vanished, an eternity ago, the day before yesterday. She felt the blood rushing through her veins, took a deep breath and held it while she knocked as loudly as her fist would allow. It hurt.

She exhaled.

Waited.

Nothing.

Eleanor gave it another moment before turning away, awash with relief.

Just then, she heard the squeaky hinges of a back door being opened, followed by shuffling footsteps, accompanied by a series of deep phlegmy coughs, betraying decades of smoking tobacco.

It's not him.

Whereas the thought of having to look into those amber eyes again had been scary enough, the realisation that she had just summoned a complete stranger *(of the older generation by the sound of it)* induced sheer panic. But she couldn't leave before the gate was opened.

It would be rude.

"Hang on," a rough voice said behind the gate in between more coughs. Eleanor could smell the distinct scent of Old Holborn now, Luke's favourite.

A dead bolt was being moved on the other side and the gate was partially opened to reveal a man in his seventies, leaning heavily on a walking stick, smouldering roll up sticking to his lower lip.

The similarities were somehow obvious yet not uncanny. The same stature but bent by the years. The same kind face but less broad with a somewhat finer bone structure and an entirely different skin tone. Also, if this one had once borne freckles they had by now been accumulated into a general leatheriness that spoke of a lifetime spent outdoors. The same badly cut hair, only less thick and white with a widow's peak.

The eyes, however, were entirely different. They were grey and had a twinkle in them as they looked at her with respectful curiosity. He unstuck the roll up from his lip, dropped it and stepped on it.

"Hi there young lady," he coughed, "'scuse me."

He carried on coughing, extracted a handkerchief from a pocket and turned away from her to spit into it before putting it back.

"Sorry about that," he said more clearly now but still shaking from the effort, "Disgusting, I know. – You must be Eleanor. He said to send you over to the barn. He's waiting for you there," he nodded, "See you later."

He shut the gate again.

She heard him shuffle off.

With every step across the field her heart started pounding louder and on more than one occasion she wanted to turn and run.

But she persevered.

Nothing and nobody, she heard Ebony's words echo in her ears and distracted herself by wondering how the tall girl was faring, whether she'd made it home alright and had got her 'mini hack' in, whatever that was.

Before she knew it, she'd arrived at the barn - a building she had been aware of but hadn't paid much attention to so far. Now, with the double doors wide open she realised that it was of quite a substantial size. Outside, to the front and sides, a concrete slab had been poured, creating an area of hard standing, where the pony was currently tied up to one of a number of rings.

Pike was crouching beside the little mare, holding the front right hoof up and working around it with a large metal file. Fresh horn dust lay scattered around the other three hooves. It was clearly heavy work and the pony was presently trying to lick the sweat off his neck to a tune of gentle, not very forceful, reprimands from the boy.

"Would you mind, I'm trying to work here. – Get off, that tickles."

Eleanor stopped some distance away and watched him work, unsure as to whether either of them had clocked her or not.

There was something timeless and ancient about the picture they painted and also something of a whole, that made Eleanor feel like an intruder. As he stood up half way, still bent over, using the file like a ruler across the length and width of the hoof, evidently to check on his work, Eleanor took a step back, ready to exit quietly.

"Oh no, you don't," he said loudly, his head shooting up to look straight at her.

There they were again. Those eyes.

And there was one of those shivers again, just like the first time she'd trudged up the path. A shiver that stayed deep inside, lodged between stomach and hips.

"I'm doing this purely for your benefit - always better to ride on even feet - no chickening out now," he smiled as he let go of the hoof, straightened up, patted The Mouse on the neck and came towards her.

Coming to a halt in front of her, he took his T-shirt off to reveal more tone-in-tone freckles and mopped his forehead with it before slinging it across his neck. Catching Eleanor's eyes wander over his body, he grinned.

"Fair is fair," he stretched out a hand, "Come, I'll give you the tour."

Eleanor hesitated. It had taken a moment for her to cotton on to what he'd meant and now she felt awkward, self conscious and mildly scared again, acutely aware that she was standing in a deserted field, with a much older boy *who had been watching her* and who was holding a massive slab of metal in one hand, while offering the other to take her into a deserted building.

Classic.

Reading her thoughts, a frown came over his face as his eyes narrowed and the amber suddenly turned mahogany red. He leant forward, inches from her face, closer than he had at the bus stop. His voice took on an angry edge.

"How old are you?" It sounded almost like a challenge.

Eleanor held his gaze.

"Fourteen next Tuesday."

"Exactly," he tried to cover up his surprise, "I'm sixteen. So even *if* I was the kind of person who was into a quick fuck and even *if* I was interested in you and even *if* you consented, it would be statutory rape. And trust me, the *last* thing I need right now on top of everything else is any trouble with the law. I don't even break the fucking speed limit in a twenty zone. So chill. Stop being so fucking paranoid. I told you, I'm not gonna eat you."

He straightened up again, his eyes back to amber and held out his hand a second time.

This time Eleanor took it.

As she felt his coarse palm close around hers, she realised with a heart stopping jolt what it had been she'd been so scared of.

Total trust.

There was absolutely nowhere, she wouldn't have gone with him.

Chapter 11

The barn turned out to be huge, holding twelve large loose boxes, six on either side, hay storage, and a tack room big enough to have a shabby old sofa under a Perspex window and a series of lockers.

Sticking out from the wall opposite the sofa were a dozen empty wooden saddle arms with hooks underneath where the bridles would have hung.

But bar one saddle arm and bar one box (*'Blueberry Mouse'* the name plate read), everything and everywhere was empty, cleaned out and spotless. Even all the other name plates had been removed, leaving holes where the screws had been.

Although Eleanor had never set foot in a stable yard before, or had any idea what it was supposed to be like, she could sense the desertedness, the utter wrongness of it all.

Too clean.

Once upon a time there would have been life here.

Now there was only emptiness.

It felt like a ghost town, in which the little pony, who'd followed them in, having been untied by Pike on the way, and the boy were rattling around.

Remnants of old.

"What happened here?" Eleanor asked.

They were standing with their backs to the tack room door, looking out onto the aisle between the boxes, where The Mouse was ambling around aimlessly, sniffing at some bars here and there. Pike rummaged around in his jeans pockets and extracted a grey-brown lump of something that smelled intensely of mint.

"Here, Blue," he called quietly and the pony ambled over to gently take the treat off his flat palm with her soft lips. After she'd munched through it, she snuggled her forehead against his tummy and let him scratch behind her ears. The action was absentminded, his eyes still set on the emptiness of the barn and as Eleanor glanced over at him, she thought she could see tears forming in his eyes. For an instant she felt transported back, yet again, to the first time she'd walked up the path, to that wasteland of grief that had made her feet feel like they were stuck in treacle. There was a desertedness and despair about him that tugged at her heart strings and made her want to scoop him up in a big hug.

Yeah. That would be effective, she thought cynically, *all four foot three of me, clinging to his waist. That'll make him feel safe.*

Instead, she tried to ask a different question.

"I thought she was called The Mouse?"

"She is now," he replied automatically, still not taking his eyes out of the past, while simultaneously glancing down at the pony, "as in 'The Mouse that got left behind'. There were two. Blueberry and Strawberry – blue and red roans, same height, same gait. Beautiful. We used to ride pas de deux with them. We rocked," he shrugged then turned to Eleanor, "Come on, I take it you didn't bring anything. We need to kit you out if you want to ride."

She didn't move.

"Pike?" it was the first time she'd called him by his name and it felt strange.

"Uhu?"

She took a deep breath.

"I've never sat on a horse before."

He raised his eyebrows, looking at her with genuine surprise.

"But…" then he laughed loudly, cupped the pony's head in his palms and raised it up to lean his forehead against the mare's, "Oh my word, Blue, we got ourselves a beginner."

56

About half an hour later, Eleanor was standing in the middle of the schooling area behind the barn, looking across The Mouse's naked back, her own tummy touching the side of the pony's, left foot raised in the air, the way Pike had just shown her.

Her head was still spinning with all the information she'd absorbed in the last half an hour, while being shown how to groom the little pony who - as she had learned upon asking what '14.1 on tippy toes' meant - was only 12 hands. Not very tall, according to Pike, although presently Eleanor would have liked to differ – if she'd had enough saliva left in her mouth to talk with. She was shaking with nerves and Pike who'd just cupped her raised shin in his right hand, while with the other holding on to the lead rope fastened to the pony's headcollar, looked at her inquisitively from the side.

"Are you ready?"

"No."

"On you get then," he grinned and gave her a lift from under the shin. Eleanor automatically pushed herself off and as she heard him demand, "swing the other leg over," did as she was told.

Suddenly she was sitting astride the pony, feeling the warmth of her back through the thin fabric of Pike's old jodhpur trousers. *('I can't believe you were once this tiny.'* – *'I wasn't born sixteen, silly.')*

Eleanor held her breath as she felt a rush of love shooting from the pony's body, into her legs and up to her heart. It was the strangest, most wonderful sensation she'd ever experienced in her life. It was like the hug the pony had given her the morning she'd first come to visit - only stronger and more direct, not from the outside but from within.

She beamed at Pike.

He smiled back knowingly.

"You ready?" he asked matter-of-factly.

"Uhu."

"Ok. I'm gonna put a hand on your thigh, just to steady you. Is that alright?"

"Yup," she was still too overwhelmed to be anything more than monosyllabic.

"Right, if you fall, you fall into my arms. Now grab yourself some mane like this," he showed her how.

"Doesn't that hurt her?" she asked as she was doing it.

"Not if you grab a chunk large enough. It's like pulling people's hair. You can pull a whole pigtail evenly and it doesn't hurt – but if you catch only a few hairs, it stings like hell," he grinned, "Not that I'm in the habit of pulling girls' pigtails. – Right," he put his hand on her thigh, "pull in your tummy muscles, shoulders back, sit nice and straight, *look* forward but don't fall forward. Good. Now brace your back, give her a tiny, and I mean tiny, squeeze with you buttocks and your legs – here we go."

They had started walking.

At first Eleanor felt wobbly but with Pike's reassuring hand on her leg, she got into the rhythm of the pony's walk quite quickly and after half a round circling the schooling paddock, he took the hand away.

"Right, you got balance. That's the most important thing in horse riding. – Don't let your body fall forward though."

"It's difficult, holding on to the mane. I can't do that and sit straight at the same time. It's not possible," Eleanor argued.

Pike laughed.

"I know. - Let go of the mane then."

"And hold on to what exactly?"

"Nothing. The whole point is that you're not holding on to anything. Like I said, balance. Horse riding is all about balance."

He glanced at her over his shoulder, challenge in his eyes. She let go of the mane and put her arms out to the side, like a tight rope walker.

"Better?" she asked.

"Very good," he replied, "although, that was going to be the next exercise. First I was going to get you to stretch just one arm out. But since you're jumping the gun – you ready?"

"For what?"

"This," he replied, putting the hand back on her thigh before clicking his tongue a few times. The pace and rhythm underneath Eleanor changed in an instant and her arms came down as she felt herself being catapulted up and down on the trotting pony, nearly sliding off, towards Pike who was running along sideways. The grip on her thigh got harder, almost pushing her back into position as he gave her instructions: "Keep those tummy muscles pulled in, *don't* fall forward. Try to let your hips go with the motion."

She did as she was told. For a moment she found just the right position, her bum glued to the pony's back as her pelvis moved with the rhythm but she lost it again almost as quickly and found herself bouncing on the pony's spine once more.

Poor Mouse, she thought, *that can't be nice for her.*

In the same moment, Pike uttered a low "whoa" and they all went back to a walk.

"Surely *that* does hurt her though," Eleanor stated breathlessly.

"If you don't manage to keep your bottom on the pony, yes, it does. But you did well there. You had the rhythm for a moment. Now for the next few years the objective is to learn to *keep* that rhythm," he grinned, "Now, what do you reckon, the most important thing in horse riding is?"

"Balance?" Eleanor offered with a sly smile.

"Funny. No, I mean, what's the most useful thing to know?"

"How to stay on?"

"Yup, that's generally quite useful but knowing how to fall is equally as important. - No, that isn't what I meant either."

"Errr, how to steer?"

During their exchange he had stopped the mare, clicked off the lead rope and was currently turning it into a make shift set of reins by fastening it left and right to the headcollar.

"Almost. – Here," he put the reins into her hands, threading them through little and ring finger then folding her fist around them and turning them upwards "and put the thumb on top of the reins. There. Now she can't pull them through your fists. If you have the thumb to the side of the reins, she can just pull them through and take the reins away from you. Here, don't lock your elbows. They should be practically by the side of your body. If you lock them you have no leverage and if you get into a tug-of-war, the horse has already won. Not that you need much leverage for this one, she stops on a breath. *Normally.* But there is no such thing as a clockwork pony. They are sentient beings, one day you might need that leverage."

As he was talking Eleanor suddenly realised that he had done this many, many times before. The patter was well oiled, schooled by somebody else who he was emulating. "Hey, you still with me?" he looked up at her, "No, the most important thing to know is how to stop the bloody thing."

And for the rest of the lesson, until Pike's old riding hat, which was marginally too tight for her, felt like it was boring through her temples, Eleanor learned just that.

"Breathe in through the nose, out through the belly button, make yourself sit deep and heavy, hug the pony with your legs, lightly pull the reins towards you. – Now, all at the same time." - She could still hear his voice as she went to sleep that night, aching all over from using muscles she had never known she had and happier than she'd ever been before.

Chapter 12

Eleanor's bliss (and muscle aches) lasted until the following Friday but as the weekend and with it the holidays drew nearer, she realised that inventing lies to get out of the house on her own every afternoon was a finite art.

Already Isabel had started making noises about wanting to meet this infamous 'Mouse' person, whether that person was allowed to visit other people's houses or not. She had questioned Eleanor at great length as to whether 'these folks' were religious nutcases or what other reason there could be that this girl was allowed to have friends over but not vice versa.

Eleanor suspected that the only reason her mum didn't think anything sinister was going on was that Eleanor couldn't possibly suppress the glow of happiness. She also reckoned that if she'd been more of a normal-sized teenager her mum would have long asked her whether there was a boy in the mix. As it went, the thought had apparently not even crossed Isabel's mind, which actually mildly annoyed Eleanor.

Although Eleanor wasn't so sure about Kjell. Occasionally she caught him looking at her across the dinner table, cocking his head and narrowing his eyes as if he harboured ideas much closer to the truth. But he never probed.

So far, Eleanor's success in perpetuating the lie had largely depended on luck. More midwife appointments (she was sure now that something wasn't entirely right with the baby, why on earth would one have a midwife appointment *every* frigging day if everything was fine? – so much for secrets); Isabel being exhausted and needing to sleep; an old friend in town for recording at Jon's popping in for a cup of tea, had all played neatly into her hand so far.

But on Friday, as she was cycling up the path in the torrential rain that had decided to grace most of the South coast, she couldn't ignore a terrible sense of foreboding.

It didn't get better when she turned up in the barn, soaked to the bones and squelching in her Wellingtons, to find a depressed Mouse standing, head hanging low, in the aisle of the stable block, while listening to Pike murdering 'The Ballad of Serenity' on a badly tuned guitar in the tack room.

Eleanor smiled.

She hadn't heard the song since Luke had left, taking his sci-fi collection with him. The Christmas before that, Isabel and Eleanor had recorded an extended version of it, just for him, with Eleanor singing and playing the guitar to Isabel's unmistakable violin. - What were the chances?

"Hey, Mouse," Eleanor greeted the pony softly and rubbed the flat of her palm against the mare's forehead. The pony woke up momentarily, blew some air into the girl's face, nibbled gently at her jacket and then went back to assume her previous stance. Eleanor tried to rouse her again with a scratch behind the ear but when she found there was nothing doing left the pony to her melancholy.

Instead, she approached the tack room door quietly and remained standing in the door frame, her heart making a leap, as it did every day when she first saw him – usually here and not at school, where their paths rarely crossed.

It was a strange thing.

After the first glimpse, which would always come with an inexplicable bolt of fear, she'd feel as safe and contented around him as could be. She trusted him completely, whether it'd be on the ground or when she was on the pony and he was teaching her, pushing her a bit further every time. He had taught her so much in only four days. She could walk the pony around on her own now, off the lead rein, steering with her weight and her legs on a long rein and stopping her beautifully. The last couple of days, they'd been trying more short bursts of trotting and when she got it right, Eleanor loved the sensation. Occasionally she'd ask herself whether Pike had other friends and where he would have been if he hadn't been here, with her, every day.

They had settled into a routine. After riding they would collect the manure from the field together. (*'Got to keep it nice and clean for worm control. Besides, would you want to eat where you shit? In the wild they can just move on and come back when the shit's turned to earth.'*)

Come seven o'clock they would feed The Mouse. (*'She doesn't really need feeding with all this grass to herself but she needs supplements these days.'*)

Afterwards Eleanor would cycle home and he would trail her on the motorbike till they got to her house, then he'd zoom past to wherever he was going that night.

A couple of nights she had seen him from her window, coming back an hour or so later, the little Yamaha - the engine noise of which she could have picked out of a million others by now - laden with groceries. Another night he had been gone for hours and Eleanor had felt an undefined fear until she could finally hear the little bike go past the house in the other direction, back home.

All she knew was he cared for his grandfather who'd had a stroke some time ago and with whom he lived alone in the house opposite. She hadn't been inside it or met the old man again since their initial encounter or knew what had happened to Pike's parents. Her guess was that they had died in a traffic accident because she'd overheard Tinkerbelle talking about him to someone at school and referring to 'since the crash' but it could have meant anything.

Talking of car crashes, she thought as he launched into another, equally tuneless, rendition of 'Serenity'.

"Hey," she shouted over the noise, "leave that poor song alone."

For the first time ever he'd been so absorbed in what he was doing, he hadn't notice her approach and he looked up startled.

"You came!" The air of despondency lifted as he beamed at her.

Eleanor took a moment to understand. Then she laughed, "Rain or shine, you said. Every day, you said. You didn't think I'd let you have all the fun of poo-picking in the rain to yourself, did you? I take it there is no riding today. Come on, get your flippers on."

Half a wheelbarrow later, they were back in the tack room, totally drenched. Pike was rummaging through a locker on the hunt for dry clothes, while Eleanor was sitting on the edge of the sofa, tuning the guitar, trying not to drip water on it.

Pike looked at her sceptically over his shoulder.

"Careful with that. Do you know what you're doing? - You don't even have a tuning fork."

"Hm," Eleanor mumbled, "don't need one."

He handed her a pair of lady's jodhpurs and a holey jumper.

"Here. They were Karen's, they'll be way too baggy but they shouldn't be massively too long at least. The others are in the wash."

In the event, Eleanor still had to roll the trousers up five times and use a lead rope as a belt, while the jumper ended just above her knees - but it was nice to be dry. Pike, who'd left her to get changed on her own and who presently came back from the stable dressed in a different pair of jeans and new T-shirt, looked at her in surprise, "Funny, I forget how tiny you are."

"Thanks," Eleanor replied sarcastically, although secretly she was pleased. She looked down at herself and wondered who this Karen was, whose smell she had got a faint whiff off as she had pulled the jumper over her head.

"Don't be sarky. Count yourself lucky," he replied, "I'd give anything to still be able to ride Blue."

There was something Eleanor had noticed over the past few days: whenever he referred to the pony in relation to her she was The Mouse but between him and the mare she was 'Blue' and nothing else.

"Hm," Eleanor replied, then suddenly took heart, "Who is this Karen? Whose clothes am I wearing?"

He looked at her mildly stunned then faked a West Country accent.

"That's right, you're not from round these parts, are you?" He stopped, cleared his throat and sat down on the sofa, picking up the guitar again. "Karen's my aunt. She…ran this place. Now she doesn't."

"Is she…?" Eleanor didn't know how to ask without it sounding stupid.

"Dead? - No. In Scotland. Breeding Friesian ponies or Dales horses, Fales or Driesians, the verdict's still out on that. They haven't had the first foal yet."

It went right over her head but she felt like they were on a roll, so she let it go, concentrating on him.

"What about your parents?"

"What about them?"

"Are they…."

"Dead? - No. In London. Saving the fucking world. Single-handedly. It all rests on their shoulders, I'll have you know. I wish they were sometimes. Would make our life a hell of a lot easier," he wiped his brow violently then looked up at Eleanor, "Don't look so shocked. I don't mean it. Well, I say that…." he smiled, "you ever read Cat's Cradle? No, of course not. You're only thirteen. Nobody reads Cat's Cradle at thirteen. Anyway, it's this book by a guy called Kurt Vonnegut. Brilliant writer. It's kind of a sci-fi, only it isn't really. It's about the end of the world. Only it isn't really. It's about religion. Only it isn't really. Anyway, beside the point, he comes up with this concept, right, of a karass. Which is basically all the people you meet in life that somehow you belong with for no discernible reason other than that you do. Like you are in my karass. And then there is the perverted version of this, which is when the karass consists of only two people and that's called a duprass. And the worst is when the duprass consists of a man and a woman in a relationship together. To the exclusion of all others. And that's my parents. They are like the most intense duprass you can possibly imagine. Even worse, they're like the most intense duprass you can possibly imagine on a mission to save the frigging world by finding a complete cure for AIDS. That's it, that's their remit in life. And everything else is a sideline. And you can't even argue with it, cause it's so fucking *noble*."

As he'd talked himself first into a rage and now back into despondency, he'd started strumming the guitar again. Eleanor grabbed it from him.

"Oh, no you don't," she said resolutely, "allow me."

And then she sang for him.

After she'd finished he looked at her through those amber eyes for a long, long time.

"Fuck me," he said quietly.

One day, Eleanor dead-panned in her head, then broke eye contact as she blushed and looked down at her hands.

"Man, you're good. Don't get me wrong but that's probably the sexiest, saddest thing I've heard in my *life*. Where did you learn to play like that? How can you *sing* like that? Uhar," he shuddered and cleared his throat, "Wow. - I think maybe it's time to take you home now."

Chapter 13

"So, would it be okay if I disappeared after lunch? Go over to Mouse's?"

Eleanor, Isabel and Kjell were sitting at the breakfast table, carving up the day's chores. Eleanor had just volunteered to do not only the floors, which Isabel found extremely heavy work these days, but also to do the bathrooms, so she thought it would be reasonably safe to ask.

"No," came her mother's abrupt reply. There was an edge to it already.

"What do you mean, no?" Eleanor asked, doing her best wide-eyed impression.

"I mean, no. I'm not having it. I want to meet this person now. You've spent every single day this week there and I have no idea who this is. Invite them here. You're not leaving this house."

"But…"

"No buts," Isabel glowered at her, "Eleanor, you're the worst liar under the sun. I have no idea what it is you've been up to but you are not leaving this house again until you tell me the truth!"

The doorbell rang and as Kjell rose to answer it, Isabel put a hand on his arm and heaved herself out of her chair, "It's Ebony. I'll go."

"Ebony?" Eleanor shouted after her mum.

"Yeah. She's come back for the weekend. She's staying here. They messed up one of the tracks, it needs rerecording," her mum answered, her voice growing louder as she moved off down the hallway.

Kjell looked at Eleanor, a friendly gleam in his eyes.

"You could just own up to her, you know," he began quietly, "I'm not entirely sure why horse riding is such a big secret anyway. - Unless it's something to do with the boy on the Yamaha."

Eleanor was stunned.

"How? How do you know?"

Kjell smiled.

"You smell of horse, Eleanor. Every night you come home. Hell, you smell of horse *now*. Isabel can't smell it but I can."

"Oh."

"I don't mind. I like it. It makes the house smell like a home and not a dentist's practice. - I used to ride."

"I know," Eleanor let slip.

"I know, you know."

Eleanor frowned at him inquisitively.

"You put the book back in the wrong place."

"No I didn't."

"Yes you did," he grinned, "It belongs one further to the left. Don't worry, I don't mind. Books are there to be read. You can borrow a book any time you like. As long as you put it back. Although this one is special, of course."

"Are you famous?"

He laughed.

"I'm not, no. My mother was, a little bit. She was a photographer. When it meant something. Before digital. – I think you should tell her."

"Tell me what?" demanded Isabel who had returned to the kitchen, dragging a heavily laden Ebony behind her.

"Hi Ebony," Eleanor said quietly.

"Hi Elle," the older girl replied, "good to see you."

She'd managed to make the latter half of the sentence sound more like 'what the hell have I walked into', prompting Kjell to get up, introduce himself and offer to show her to her room.

Isabel and Eleanor were left alone in the kitchen, sizing each other up.

"Tell me what?" Isabel demanded again.

"I'll tell you, when you tell me what's wrong with the baby," Eleanor said coldly.

Isabel sat down heavily and sighed.

"It's got a heart murmur."

"I see, and you accuse me of lying? Nice one."

"Your go."

"I've been going horse riding."

"You have what?" It was clear that of all the answers Isabel might have expected this one had not been among them.

"I've been going over to see the pony by the twitten every day and I've been learning to ride on her. She's called Mouse," Eleanor stated matter-of-factly.

"What?" Isabel was still totally confused, "But…who's been teaching you?"

"A boy called Peter. She used to be his pony but he is too tall for her now."

"A *boy?*" Isabel's voice rose in anger, "You've been horse riding with some *boy* teaching you, not even a proper instructor? What on earth were you *thinking?* It's dangerous. Is this person charging you for it? Did you at least wear a helmet?"

I knew it. I knew she wouldn't understand.

"Yes, mum, I've been wearing a helmet. And no, he's not charging me and he's actually a very good instructor. The best."

Eleanor could feel tears of anger welling up in her eyes.

"Right. Enough of this. It ends here. You're grounded. If you want to have proper horse riding lessons with a proper instructor at a proper riding school, we can talk about it. Maybe. Once you are ungrounded. - In about a month."

This was so typically her mother. For all her cool, for all her dope smoking and living the musician's life, at the end of the day she remained a girl school violin prodigy, who insisted all learning was done 'properly' and by the book. Eleanor didn't know what to do. She had never been grounded before. The last time she'd been sent to her room even had been around the age of eight. She remembered it clearly because the room in question had been a tepee.

She shot her mother a glance, got up quietly and – heart pounding in her chest – walked past her, down the hall, to the pile of shoes by the front door. She was still in her PJs but they would have to do. They were black, raw silk – an early birthday present from Jerry that had arrived from Australia in the post a couple of days previously, undoubtedly picked out by his current girlfriend who was part Indonese. It could have been worse. She slipped her black Converse on, opened the door and left the house. She would have to walk it, her bike was still around the back.

The entire way she expected Kjell to pull up next to her (her mum had finally stopped driving altogether) and each time a car approached from behind, her heart quickened. But they didn't come.

Finally she reached the garden gate of Pike's house (she still hadn't worked out where the front entrance was), knocked heavily and waited. When nothing happened she began pounding the gate, kicking it and calling his name – until he opened up, wearing a tatty, untied old man's bathrobe over a pair of boxer shorts.

"Whoa, whoa, whoa," he said, snatching her still pounding fists mid-air and holding her by the wrists, "easy, girl."

"I'm not a horse," she stated, sniffling, smiling at him through the tears that had been streaming down her face continuously since she'd left her house.

"No, you're not. You're a mess. – Come in."

He pulled her through the gate and shut it behind her.

"Oh, man, Eleanor, really?" Pike was looking at her sideways, head in hands, utter despair but also annoyance in his voice.

They were sitting around the kitchen table in his house, which was clean but cluttered to the hilt, instantly making Eleanor feel at home here. His Grandfather, who had introduced himself as Aaron, was standing by the Aga, in the process of brewing loose leaf tea in a china tea pot that looked like it had already survived both World Wars and then some. The smell of Assam began floating through the kitchen, mingling with the pervading smell of Old Holborn and the residue of the cooked breakfast, which Eleanor had interrupted with her arrival. Eleanor who was sitting on the short side of an L-shaped bench had drawn up her legs and was hugging her knees, chin on top, looking apologetically at Pike, sitting on the long side.

"I'm sorry."

"I told you I can't have any trouble right now. I thought they knew. Or at least didn't care. - Fuck."

"Language!" Aaron reprimanded him from the Aga then burst into a coughing fit. When he was finished, he took the strainer out of the pot, shuffled to the table and began pouring tea into mugs in front of them.

"Thank you," Eleanor said quietly, looking up at the old man.

Pike was staring into his mug as if it could provide him with answers, until his phone vibrated on the table. He picked it up, looked at the display, excused himself and left the room. The old man sat down and began rolling a cigarette.

"I'm sorry," Eleanor repeated, this time to him, "I didn't mean to make your life difficult."

He looked at her over the roll up as he dragged his tongue along the gum strip, then his face broke into a warm smile.

"Don't you worry, little lady, difficult is what we do best around here. And don't you let him make you feel like you're a burden. You're the best thing that's happened to him since the accident, make no mistake. I haven't seen him this alive in a long time. There was a point when I

72

thought he was broken for good but that's all changed in the last week. I think he might even start fighting for his life and his land again and that's worth a whole bunch of trouble with your parents, trust me," he winked at her, lit the cigarette, took a drag and went into another coughing fit. "I just wish I could be more use to him," he pressed out between coughs.

"Maybe it would help if you stopped smoking you old fool," Pike said as he walked back into the room, fully clothed now.

"Sod off," the old man coughed.

"Language!" Pike retorted, then turned to Eleanor, "Come on, I'm going to take you back home."

Eleanor's heart sank.

Chapter 14

They had walked the entire way in silence, hand in hand. It made her feel partly like a naughty child being marched back to the shopkeeper it stole from and partly utterly protected, like always when she was with him. Before they'd set off, Eleanor had tried to convince him to give her a lift on the Yamaha but he'd flat out refused.

"If they don't want you on my pony, I'm sure as hell not gonna deliver you back on a motorbike. Besides, I haven't got a lid for you," was the last thing that had been said between them until now, half a street away from Eleanor's house.

Pike squeezed her hand lightly a couple of times and stopped.

He's going to leave me here, Eleanor thought, *I'm going to have to crawl back on my own.*

Instead, he sat down on a garden wall to be at eye level with her, took both her hands into his and stroked the back of them lightly with his thumbs, his long legs stretched out left and right of her. Then he looked up at her.

"I need to tell you something before we go in. That…was Karen on the phone," he let go of her hands, steeling himself, looking over her shoulder into the distance, "She's coming down for the September auctions and then she is going to take The Mouse with her."

"What?" Eleanor didn't understand.

"She was only left behind out of commitment to the last of our liveries. As a companion. Horses are herd animals, they need other horses, or at least one other horse. You can't keep them on their own, they go – well, like she's gone now, you know. Sad and lonely. Some go crazy, mean even. The Mouse wouldn't but it's not fair on her. Karen was going to pick her up the week before you turned up but the horse they were interested in down here was sold elsewhere, so it didn't happen."

Slowly Eleanor started comprehending what was being said and she felt her insides turn into a lump of ice.

"No! No, no, no," Eleanor couldn't think of anything else to say and started sobbing again, looking at him in despair, "We'll get another," she suggested after a while, fully aware of the absurdity of the idea, "one you can ride."

He snorted a laugh and put a hand behind her head, his little and ring finger resting lightly in the nape of her neck as he pulled her towards him to rest his forehead against hers. He didn't release her when he spoke, looking down, addressing the floor.

"That's not going to happen, Eleanor. Don't listen to what the old man said. She is going. The land is going. The question is," he let go of her, grabbed her by the shoulders now and looked deep into her soul, "do you want to keep us company until it happens? - I can understand if you don't want to get more involved. It will hurt like hell. Like no pain you have ever experienced. Death is easy compared to saying goodbye to a pony you love. Your choice. But I need to know *now*. Before I go in there and meet your parents, cause it'll change how I go in."

Eleanor smiled. All she could think of was that he had never planned on leaving her here. And somehow, instinctively, she knew that as long as The Mouse hadn't gone yet there was hope, much as he pretended otherwise. She took a step forward, slung her arms around him and nestled her face into the crook of his neck.

"Of course, I do," she mumbled against his skin, "I'll keep you company for as long as you'll have me."

A shiver went through the boy and as he hugged her back she could feel the power shift, could feel him sink into her arms, looking for strength, protection and…hope. She tried to give back as much as she could, crawling deeper into him, his long legs closing around her. Through the silk of her pyjama's she could feel his heart beating fast against hers before he abruptly let go of her, grabbing her by the shoulders again.

"You've got to stop doing that," he implored, his eyes closer to mahogany again.

"Doing what?"

He shot her a look, ran a hand through his hair and stood up.

"Right. Let's do this."

It was almost like a magic trick.

She could feel him assume more authority with every step closer to the house and by the time he pushed the door bell, he was that person again, who had the power to dismiss a bus driver with one small gesture.

Nevertheless, Eleanor was relieved when Kjell and not her mother opened the door. Pike offered a hand.

"I'm Peter."

Kjell looked at the hand in impressed surprise, before he took and shook it. He often complained about the oddity of the British ritual around introduction, being such a big deal yet half the time not including such a simple, straight forward action as a handshake. He invited Pike in and when on top of the handshake the boy took his shoes off in the hallway without having to be asked, Eleanor knew he'd already won the older man over. Eleanor could see down the hall that her mum was still in the kitchen, sitting with her back to the door, pretty much in the same position Eleanor had left her in. She hadn't turned around. Ebony had assumed Eleanor's place at the table and was talking to Isabel in a low voice, a mug cupped in her hands.

Kjell led them to the kitchen. Eleanor hung behind in the doorway as Kjell beckoned Pike to come in.

"Isabel, Ebony – this is Peter," Kjell introduced them.

"Pleased to meet you," Pike said and held out a hand to Isabel.

76

There was an awkward moment when she didn't take it and although Eleanor could only see her back from where she was, she knew, could *feel*, that Isabel was looking him up and down in disgust. She briefly looked over her shoulder to glance at Eleanor coldly, then back at Pike. "Thank you for bringing her back," she stated matter-of-factly, "That's very decent of you. I'm sure Eleanor has told you that she's grounded. So there'll be no more pony related shenanigans. And if - "

She didn't get further because suddenly Ebony, who'd been watching the scene unfold quietly through narrowed eyes stuck firmly on Pike, started coughing tea out of her nose, turning the scene into a flurry of people fetching kitchen roll for her face and a dishcloth for the table. Through coughs and air swallowing she was pointing a hectic finger at him.

"Oh – my – word. I *do* know you," she'd composed herself looking at him astonished, "You are Peter Pike." He looked at her, taken aback and thrown out of context, brows furrowed.

"Don't worry," Ebony continued, laughing shyly, "you wouldn't remember me. I'm just a mere mortal."

A flicker of recognition passed over the boy's face and he smiled, pointing back at her jovially.

"Bridgewater Kelpie," he burst out, "You have to forgive me, I never remember riders' names. I only ever remember the horses'."

"Oh my word," Ebony repeated, still stunned, "I thought you were dead or something. What happened to you? I always think of you whenever I see Tinkerbelle Jones' name crop up somewhere. She still competes - but she's crap without you and the Mice. She's quite a bit younger than you isn't she? Still, she's got this massive German Warmblood now. All muscles and legs. Way outhorsed. - Sorry, I didn't mean to offend. I guess you're still friends?"

"Not remotely. No offence taken," he smiled at her warmly and Eleanor could feel a stab in her heart.

Great. Pike, meet the Goddess. Ebony, meet... God? What had she meant by that comment about being a mere mortal? What...?

The thought was aborted because now Ebony was addressing Eleanor over the head of the stone statue that was her mother.

"This is your riding instructor?" she asked in awe.

Eleanor nodded.

"And, oh my word, the penny drops, which Mouse? Tell me, which Mouse?" She was looking back at Pike now clapping her hands like an overzealous seal.

"Blueberry," he answered amusedly.

"I hate you," Ebony smiled at Eleanor, "You must be the jammiest cow alive. You're being taught horse riding by Peter Pike on Blueberry Mouse. I can't believe it."

"Oh no, she is not," Isabel heaved herself out of her chair and stood with her back to the fridge so as to be able to see all those present in the room. Her eyes wandered from Eleanor, to Kjell, to Pike, to Ebony and back to Eleanor. Her face had not softened. On the contrary, her jaw was set now. Eleanor knew her mum well enough to know that she despised nothing more than the feeling of being an outsider, not in with the crowd, not in with whatever was going on. And that was exactly what was happening here. The other four people in the room had a connection she didn't, *couldn't,* share. As far as Eleanor knew, the closest her mum had ever come to a horse was watching reruns of 'Black Beauty' with her daughter when she was little.

"Thank you, young man, for bringing her back. I think it's time you left my house now. – Eleanor, go to your room, please. You *are* grounded till further notice. – Kjell, don't... - Ebony, thank you for your ear but it's time you got to the studio now."

And that was that.

Chapter 15

If anyone had told Eleanor even a week before that she could have hated her mother as much as she hated her now, Eleanor would have laughed in their face. She kept remembering a snippit from her early childhood, when Isabel had predicted that one day Eleanor wouldn't want to be hugged and cuddled by her anymore and herself replying with utter conviction, 'Never, mummy.'

Well, I guess that time has come, Eleanor thought bitterly but with a pain in her heart, each time the memory came back to haunt her.

She rolled onto her other side, facing the wall again, trying to go back to the daydream that had been interrupted by a knock on her door, which she had left unanswered.

It was day three of her incarceration, the first official day of the summer holidays, the night before her birthday and she hadn't come out of her room, other than to use the bathroom and get water, since the moment Isabel had sent her up here. At first her mum had shrugged it off, sure that Eleanor would come down eventually, once hungry enough. Having already taken her computer and telephone as part of the punishment on day one, on the second day she had confiscated her music player as well, stating she could use any technology in the house, once she'd come to the kitchen and had something to eat.

It didn't wash.

If Eleanor wanted music, she could make her own.

If Eleanor wanted to watch something, she could watch the dreams in her head.

So she'd spent the last 60 hours or so dreaming of horses and of the boy that came with them, although she tried hard to avoid focusing in on him too much. She'd had crushes before, on film stars and boys at her various schools, but this was different and she didn't want to taint their relationship by fantasising about him. There was also the notion that if she did think about him *in that way* he would somehow know, be able to feel it, a couple of miles down the road.

And he'd been very clear on that.

So she ran reruns of their actual time together and spun it further. In her mind, her mum had never found out, she was still going every day, developing her riding skills under his watchful eye, The Mouse and her becoming a real team to be reckoned with. They'd go to shows and win and Pike would become famous as her trainer, beating Tinkerbelle along the way. And somehow that would change whatever troubled him so much, would save his land. Occasionally, Ebony – who'd been and gone in reality, after sneaking into Eleanor's room in the middle of that first night to tell her a bit more about the famous double act of Peter Pike and Tinkerbelle Jones on their two roans - would come into the dreams, too.

The problem Eleanor had was that she still didn't know enough about riding, let alone showing and competing to make the daydreams remotely plausible and that her brain always seemed to frizzle out at the point where she'd tell Tinkerbelle, *'They're with me now'*.

The other problem Eleanor had was that the *last* thing on earth she'd ever want was fame, in any sphere. So she kept returning to the real memories instead. To the feeling of The Mouse's love spreading through her when she got on her back and to the embrace the pony had given her that very first day she'd gone to see her that had made her feel so totally in tune with the universe. She'd think of Pike's voice, reeling off instructions and correcting her seat, of that look in his eyes when he looked into her soul and very, very occasionally, she'd think of his fingers in the nape of her neck, the tingle that it had sent down her spine and of the hug they'd shared. She figured, she couldn't be held responsible for the real, the *sleep* dreams, which would follow on from that.

Presently that was exactly where she was trying to get to but she realised she needed a drink. She turned to the glass on the floor next to her bed. It was empty and lightly dusty around the rim. She got up onto shaky legs, picked it up and staggered to the bathroom.

The last thing she remembered before the world went black was looking at the tray of food that had been left outside her door.

When Eleanor came to, she was back in her bed, a sweet taste on her lips. Kjell was by her side, holding her head up with one hand, while dripping orange juice into her mouth from a pipette with the other.

"Ah, there we are. Hello Eleanor. Nice to have you back. Here, drink this," he gave her a glass of juice and she gulped it down, "Good. Now eat something or I will call an ambulance and have you put on a drip in hospital," there was no arguing with the no-nonsense tone he had assumed, a tone she'd never heard him use before but that was firmly rooted in his medical training, "Here, start with a piece of banana."

He had actually put a slice of banana on a fork and was holding it in front of her mouth. Eleanor looked at him. Despite feeling like she was starving, the idea of food actually seemed revolting.

This must be how anorexics feel, she thought.

"I mean it. I know it's hard to swallow your pride but right now it's just a piece of banana."

There was a gentle smile in his eyes and Eleanor complied. It was the best, most intensely flavoured piece of banana she'd ever eaten but it went gooey in her mouth and she found it hard to swallow.

She had to force it down.

"Good. Now a grape."

He pinned a grape onto the fork, same spiel.

Painstakingly, he fed her half a fruit salad, piece by piece, then made her eat some buttered toast to mop up the acid. By now, Eleanor was ravenous but Kjell forbade her to eat any more for the next hour.

"Little and often, otherwise it's all going to come out again immediately. We'll get you some soup in an hour or so."

Isabel who had been watching from the door, like a vampire that hadn't been invited over the threshold, looked across to her daughter hollow-eyed. All the resolve had melted from her. She looked like she had been crying.

"Hi mum. – How's the baby?"

"Which one?" her mum sniffled as she took half a step into the room.

Kjell winked at Eleanor, got up and left quietly, gently squeezing his woman's arm on the way out.

"Can I come in?"

Eleanor shrugged but nodded at the same time and shuffled to make space.

Isabel sat down heavily on the bed.

"I guess this is the point where you don't want cuddles from me any longer, huh?"

The woman is something else, Eleanor thought and put her arms out. *Never, mummy.*

They hugged awkwardly around the big belly.

"I'm sorry, baby."

"It's alright."

"No, it's not. It's never alright." Isabel drew back to look at Eleanor, stroking her cheek with the back of one finger. "Why did you lie to me, hon?"

Eleanor looked down, cleaning dirt from under her finger nails.

"Cause I knew you wouldn't understand."

Isabel laughed.

"What? Me not understand being into a boy? Where have you been the last fourteen years?"

"That's exactly it. It's not about him. It's about The Mouse. She needs me."

"What? The pony? *Really?* "

"Yes mum, *really*."

"Hm. And are you sure, he knows that? Cause it isn't the pony that I keep seeing passing the house. And I'm sure it wasn't a pony who came to the door this morning to give me the most astonishingly beautiful, handwritten letter, trying to sweet talk me into letting you out. I have to say, you've got taste. The boy can write. And that's one hell of an effort."

Eleanor's heart was doing somersaults. He hadn't given up on her.

"Mum, he's *sixteen*. I'm thirteen, fourteen, whatever. Point is, even *if* he was interested in me and even *if* I consented to it, it would still be statutory rape and the last thing he needs is any trouble with the law. He's got enough on his plate as it is. He was very clear about this. – What?"

Her mum was looking at her aghast.

"You *talked* about this?"

"Kind of."

"Heaven help."

Chapter 16

Having eaten properly and stayed up with her mum and Kjell to watch some mindless television before being toasted to at midnight, Eleanor slept well into the next morning. She was finally woken at 11am by Isabel bending over her bed and giving her a birthday kiss followed by a phone being shoved at her ear.

"Happy birthday, baby girl." It was Jerry. "How's my favourite daughter?"

"Only daughter," Eleanor replied.

"Far as we know," he laughed his rough, raspy laugh.

"Far as we know," Eleanor repeated.

The customary introduction over, Jerry – as always – was at a bit of a loss as to what to say to her. Eleanor could hear party noises going on in the background. It was evening in Sydney. If that was, where he was. For all she knew he could be playing a gig in Toronto or be just down the road – she didn't really follow his schedule anymore.

"Where are you dad?"

"At home. We're having a bit of a party in your honour."

Any excuse.

"That's sweet, dad. Make mine a Southern Comfort and Ginger Ale."

"Funny. – Did you like your present? Did it get there in time? Does it fit?"

"Perfectly. I'm wearing it." *Have been wearing it for days.*

"It's great. Say thank you to Lia."

If I concentrate really hard the top half still smells of him, from when we hugged.

"She'll be pleased."

Cue awkward silence, take II.

"You doing anything nice today?"

"Doubt it. I'm grounded."

"You're what?" he started laughing so hard it ended in a coughing fit, "Sorry, babe, but that's hilarious. Your mother of all people! You know what she used to do when she got grounded? She used to sneak out through the window and come and see me play then she'd play with me all night. Them were the days."

"Too much information, dad."

"Sorry. – Anyway, babe, you have yourself a nice birthday, right? Love you."

"Love you, too, dad."

There was a cake downstairs at the breakfast table, flowers, cards from her grandmother and Mick but not really any presents.

"Sorry, hon, I really didn't know what to get you this year," her mum said from across the table.

Eleanor shrugged and smiled. She felt mildly disappointed but if she was honest, she wouldn't have known what to get herself either. All her wishes were not really purchasable. And somehow it didn't really feel like it was her birthday anyway.

Her mum searched her face for a reaction then laughed. "It's a good thing you have a friend who knows *exactly* what to get you. Ta-da."

Eleanor frowned inquisitively as her mum pulled one of the empty chairs from the table, revealing a cardboard box on the seat.

Oh no. She's got me a kitten. She thinks any pet will do. Eleanor smiled as she approached the box with trepidation. She opened it carefully, expecting an animal to jump out. It was a riding hat.

Brand new and it fit perfectly.

"Any good?" Isabel looked at Eleanor almost shyly, "We can change it, if it doesn't fit."

"It's perfect," Eleanor grinned after having performed all the jumping and shaking tests, Pike had asked her to do when trying out his old one, "and it doesn't push into my temples! Magic."

But what does it mean?

She took it off, staring at the blue lining then looked straight at her mum.

"But…what does it mean, mum? - Am I having riding lessons?"

"Otherwise it would be a bit of a waste, wouldn't it?"

"But where?" she looked at her mum imploringly.

Please don't send me to some riding school. Please let me go back to them. PLEASE.

"Well, I have it on fairly good authority that one of the most talented young riders in Britain, once tipped to become a future Olympian, according to the oracle, is currently taking on one pupil and one pupil only and you appear to have been selected."

It took Eleanor a moment to understand.

She went over to her mum and slung her arms around her.

"Thank you, mum, thank you, thank you, thank you," she mumbled into her bosom, then stepped back to search her mother's face, "Must have been one hell of a letter," she stated soberly after a while.

"Oh, it was. - One hell of a letter," Isabel grinned, "and you're not getting to read it. Ever."

Chapter 17

When Eleanor would look back later on to those first days of her involvement with Hawthorne Cottage, its land and keepers, the prevailing memory was always of a feeling of the planets realigning; of time passing excruciatingly slowly through an hourglass, so that the grains of sand could run through in exactly the *correct* order. She wasn't sure that she believed in fate – or anything else for that matter – but what she did know was that once the secrecy had gone and they had obtained the permission and freedom to do as they pleased, time immediately began speeding up again and her feeling of constantly being under a microscope faded away. In hindsight, she was never quite sure whether it had been those amber eyes watching her, first from afar and then up close, that had made her feel scrutinised, or the magnifying glass of the universe itself.

She knew for certain that neither was watching her now, though, as she climbed the gate for the umpteenth time since her mum had released her nearly three weeks ago. The universe, if it indeed had ever harboured any particular interest in Eleanor, had turned its attentions elsewhere and Pike had taken his grandfather for a check up this morning. Or rather, a cab driver had taken Aaron - with Pike, who refused to step inside an enclosed vehicle, trailing the taxi on his motorbike.

Eleanor relished the idea of spending some time alone with The Mouse. Much as she loved being in Pike's company (and that was pretty much all day every day), much as she missed him as soon as they parted each evening and much as she was grateful for everything he had taught her in their short time together, she sometimes just wanted to spend time with the pony on her own. Often she would deliberately come early or sneak in when she knew he wouldn't be around or watching from his room in the sky.

Halfway across the first paddock now, she turned around to look at Hawthorne Cottage, a thoroughly misnamed monster (*yet not monstrosity* she thought with admiration) of a house, that - as she knew now - encompassed five large bedrooms - excluding the tower room - all with en suites, two downstairs toilets, a sitting room, a dining room and a lounge as well as the cluttered, cosy kitchen she'd first encountered, behind which was a scullery. It was rendered white, making its unique architectural quirk, a turret sticking out of the second floor corner at the back, look like a beacon reaching up into the sky. It was called the watchtower because from its window you could see almost every inch of the paddocks and as far across the rolling hills as the next county. Now that she knew it was there, Eleanor couldn't possibly understand how she had not noticed it until the day she had first started climbing the windy stairs to Pike's room.

She sighed, looking at it now.

What else have I missed?

She was still none the wiser as to why Pike's aunt had turned her back on house and land to live as head groom with a Scottish business man who had a fixation with producing an entirely new breed of oversized ponies or undersized horses.

What she had learned by now was, that eighteen months previously his aunt had left behind a solid guest house business, which had underpinned her passion for horses, showing and picking up snotty nosed street urchins (Aaron's words) who would otherwise not have got a look in, where the expensive world of equestrianism was concerned. And Eleanor had realised - with a certain amount of anger towards the unknown woman - that the same way she had just left a lonely Mouse with one last horse on livery rattling around in a barn big enough for twelve, she'd left Pike and Aaron rattling around in a house they couldn't possibly fill on their own. Most of Hawthorne Cottage felt empty and deserted, almost spooky, when you treaded outside kitchen and lounge, where Aaron had been put up to save him from hobbling up and down the stairs too much, and Pike's room in the watchtower.

Looking up at the dark windows now, Eleanor sighed again then turned away from the building to go and locate The Mouse.

She found her in her favourite spot, a particular dip in the land, lying on her side, fast asleep in the morning sun. Contrary to popular belief, Pike had explained to her the first time she'd seen the pony in this position and started running because she thought she was injured or – worse - dead, horses *did* lie down to sleep. Being prey animals, however, they rarely elected to do so in the company of humans, who - no matter whether the horse normally regarded them as friend or foe - they instinctively responded to as predators. Hence the biggest sign of trust a horse could extend was for it to remain in that position when approached. And just about the highest accolade this particular pony could bestow upon a person was to yield to the request 'lie down'. The Mouse would do so willingly for him, of course, the same way she would perform just about any trick in the book for him.

Eleanor had seen the videos on the net by now - of a much younger, shorter and slighter version of Peter Pike and the famous Blueberry Mouse, entertaining the crowds at various high profile equestrian events with break filling trick numbers. She'd also seen clips of him and Tinkerbelle on Blueberry and Strawberry, riding breathtaking pas de deux routines *("Synchronised swimming of the horse world",* she'd explained to Isabel), easily on par with some of the internationally competing adult dressage riders on their fine, massive horses - at least to Eleanor's still entirely untrained eye.

She'd wondered, of course, what had happened to the red roan, to The Mouse That Was No More as she had secretly named her, but any attempts to try and extract that information out of him had been met with the same impenetrable stone wall that blocked all communication about the time before Eleanor. He didn't get angry whenever she asked, or sad, but there was a numb stoicism in his standard response *('Let's stick to the here and now, it'll be short enough.')* that was somehow infinitely worse than an emotional response. So she'd stopped asking.

What little she had gleaned had come from Aaron but he, too, would clam up when it came to the why-s and what happened-s to state categorically that she 'should ask Peter – it is his story to tell'.

If only he bloody well would.

She was only feet away from The Mouse now and Eleanor suddenly became aware that she was wasting their potential precious alone time, still thinking about the boy. There was something she had figured out about horses, or at least this one, without anyone telling her: it worked best when you let go of thought itself, when you let yourself just be. She tried to do that now because if there was one thing she wanted more than anything, it was for The Mouse to trust her enough not to get up. The pony, who had become aware of her presence some time ago, had opened one eye and was making a half hearted attempt at lifting the head off the ground.

"Easy girl," Eleanor whispered from where she was standing, putting one hand out, "don't get up on my account."

She slowly approached the pony, who lazily rolled onto her tummy in preparation for rising.

"I want to lie down with you."

Eleanor had crouched down now. She could just about reach the pony's nose from where she was and started stroking it. The Mouse gave a short snort. (*'Remember, if it's a long drawn out snort, it means they're contented. But little ones mean alert. A series of little snorts means very alert or very upset or both. That's when you need to be on your toes.'*)

Eleanor took the hand away and remained very still. The Mouse looked at her for a while, neither lying back down nor scrambling to her feet. Eleanor was pleased but knew enough not to get too excited or ahead of herself. Then, suddenly, she had a brainwave.

"Lie down, *Blue*," she whispered. For an instant she almost thought she could see the pony smile – before it flopped back on its side to play dead. Eleanor could have jumped for joy but instead she very slowly crawled to the pony's side to lie down next to her, resting her own head in the dip between the animal's neck and shoulder. When she had settled, she closed her eyes. A shudder of contentedness rippled through the mare's body, followed by the longest snort. Eleanor smiled to herself as she concentrated on the pony's breaths gently rising up and down underneath her, letting herself fall into this entity's all encompassing love.

And that's how he found them when he turned up.

Chapter 18

"That's the life," Pike was smiling down at them warmly but Eleanor imagined that she'd heard a hint of jealousy at the back of his throat.

It must be tough for him.

She raised herself to a sitting position and the pony rolled back onto her tummy, curling her head around Eleanor. They both looked up guiltily at the boy they shared and he started chuckling. He didn't laugh often and when he did it was usually subdued or somewhat hollow, so Eleanor was surprised to see real laughter tears forming at the corners of his eyes, as he crouched down in front of them.

"You two - we should come up with an entirely new routine where the two of you get caught stealing apples or something. The look is perfect."

He got back up to his feet, offered Eleanor his hands and pulled her up. She beat the dust off her bum.

"Could we?" she asked quietly, after a pause.

He frowned.

"Could we what?"

"Make up a new routine. - Maybe go to a show?"

"No," the answer was so short and abrupt she took a step backwards, almost bumping into the pony who had also risen in the interim and was shaking the dirt out of her coat. All joy had left him in an instant and he looked at her stony faced, his eyes verging on mahogany again. Eleanor put her hands up in a pacifying gesture.

"Whoa, easy boy. Relax."

"I'm not a horse," he replied with instantly softer eyes.

"No, you're a conundrum," she grinned but didn't let it go, "Why not?"

He sighed heavily, looking over her shoulder into the distance.

"Because we don't have the time. Or a horsebox, or a driver. Because you haven't even cantered yet. And because -" to Eleanor's surprise he didn't stop there or carry on searching the horizon but instead looked straight at her, "I don't do that anymore. Because I don't *believe* in it anymore."

"What do you mean?" she'd almost whispered it, holding his gaze, which she still found almost impossible to bear when he was burning like he was now.

"People are arseholes, Eleanor. - We make these animals go and perform tricks, make them dance and prance and jump and run and look pretty. We take them from their herds, put them in dark metal prisons on wheels, make them go here there and everywhere only to take them back in the metal prisons and then do it all over again the next week. And for *what*? For ribbons you can buy in any haberdashery store – and ego. Not even for money. Because believe me, there is no money in showing. People think there is but the prize money is a joke compared to what they pay out to get there in the first place. It's a vanity industry. Just like the rest of life. No more, no less – and I will have no part in it any longer," he broke eye contact and made a sweeping motion with his arm to encompass Eleanor, the pony, himself and the land around them, "I want to do this. - Soon I want to take you out there," he pointed beyond the hedge, "So you can see what riding is really about. And one day, realistically maybe in a couple of years or so, I want you to feel what it's like flat out galloping across a field, hearing the wind rush in your ears and your eyes watering, knowing that you are *free* and that the horse you're on is running because it's *fun,* because she's happy to be *alive* and happy to be alive *with you…*" his voice trailed off, a moment later his eyes were back on her, "But if you ever want to get that far, I'd suggest you get yourself that pony there," he nodded in the direction of the little mare who had wandered off grazing, "and get cracking."

Three quarters of an hour later Eleanor was having one of those moments when she realised once again that horse riding, as he often pointed out, was a skill that took years to learn, never to be fully accomplished.

He'd let her start trotting around the schooling area off the lead rein over the last week and was now asking her to ride the figures she'd learned at walk in trot. It took all of Eleanor's concentration to keep the rhythm, not slip and not hang onto the reins while trying to steer the pony with her weight and legs to perform to his commands, which came in rapid succession. Often, as today, there was an urgency to his teaching that made Eleanor feel rushed and flustered and then she made mistakes. Blue would normally fall back into a walk if Eleanor didn't manage to give the aids correctly, to let her sort herself out, but presently the mare had stopped altogether, nose pointing at the letter 'A' that marked the middle of the short side at the head of the arena. Having just trotted down the centre line, the pony was now thoroughly confused as to whether Eleanor was asking her to stay on the same rein, or change rein to go around in the opposite direction.

'Left or right, lady?' she seemed to ask as she bent her long neck around to look at her rider disapprovingly. Eleanor's shoulders slumped. All of a sudden she felt quite silly for suggesting that they could ever go to a show together.

"I'm sorry, Blue. I'm crap at this aren't I?" she mumbled, scratching the mare apologetically around the withers. She felt Pike's flat hand lightly pressing in between her shoulder blades as he approached from behind, having left the centre of the school from which he had been bellowing his instructions. She automatically sat up straight again, pushing her chest out.

"That's right. Never slump. Even if it doesn't work out. – And don't be silly, Eleanor. You're one of the most talented riders we've ever had…"

"Really?" she looked at him with disbelief. He'd never paid her a compliment before and it felt strange, almost awkward.

"Really," he said matter-of-factly, scratching Blue's neck while looking at Eleanor, "why do you think I'd bother otherwise, despite knowing the three of us have a limited shelf life? The first time I let you ride, I did it because you had the guts to turn up after I had a go at you..."

"But you started doing her hooves *before* I got here," she interjected. It was funny, whenever she was on the pony and he was standing next to her they were on eye level and somehow that made the exchanges easier, more equal.

"True. Details. They needed doing anyway."

He was grinning but there was also a warning in there telling her to back off that she didn't quite understand. *Don't go there.*

She focused on the mahogany specks in the amber that by now she'd discovered were always there but would inflate or deflate depending on his mood. They were flickering wildly now.

"The point is that you are very good at this Eleanor. You've got it all. The balance, the poise, the rhythm, the pelvic control *and* the empathy and you are already way ahead of where you should be. So I don't ever want to hear you saying you're crap at this, ok? You're just still a beginner. The difference between you and most people is, you're going to be a novice before this here ends, while most people will stay beginners most their riding lives. - So, what went wrong there?"

"I wasn't shifting my weight in the direction I wanted to go?"

"Worse. You were cheating. You were tipping your pelvis correctly but because you're still scared you're going to slip off, you counterweighted yourself by collapsing at the waist. You need to trust your own balance. Anyway, enough of that for today. – Are you ready?"

Eleanor had learned to become somewhat suspicious of Pike's 'are you ready'-s over the last few weeks. An 'are you ready' had preceded not only her first trot and later the request to lie down flat on her back on the pony while in walk - but also such delights as suddenly being grabbed by the wrists to be pulled off the pony by him and land pretty hard on her bottom; as well as him whistling to Blue while she was trotting on the lunge, whereupon the pony had come to such an abrupt halt that Eleanor had found herself nose-butting the mare's neck.

"Is this going to hurt?" she asked cautiously.

"Not a bit," he grinned as he led them to the middle of the arena and unclipped a lunge line from his belt, "Just remember, it's the transition back down that's the most difficult part."

"What?" she frowned.

"It's time for a canter."

"I'm not ready."

"Oh yes you are. You're just not ready to canter and steer at the same time," he clipped the lunge line onto the headcollar he customarily left on under the bridle for this very purpose and told the pony to walk on. As they started circling around him now, Eleanor's heart began beating wildly.

"Grab yourself some mane if you need to. Ask her to trot." Eleanor braced her back and gave the pony a light squeeze with her legs. Blue willingly shifted up a gear. She seemed to know what was coming because she was snorting happily in anticipation.

"Right. Now when you do go in, there'll be a moment not unlike the one you had when I made her suddenly stop. - Don't cramp up. You cramp up, you're off. After that, don't try and lean out of the circle. You've been on the back of motorbikes, you know the drill. You need to lean into the corner. And just go with the motion."

Eleanor could only half process what he was saying, adrenalin pumping through her body.

"Now, give her three light squeezes, then put your outer calf about a hand width behind the normal position, push on with the inner leg and give the inner hand forward." Blue had started trotting very fast now and Eleanor was having difficulties keeping her bum on the pony's back.

"Rein her back in, back to a nice steady trot. There we go. Now do it all again but at the same time. Squeeze, squeeze, squeeze, outer leg back, inner on, inner hand forward. And let go."

Suddenly there was a jolt underneath Eleanor and for the fraction of a second she felt suspended in time and space – before the rhythm underneath her changed and she felt herself being rocked backwards and forwards.

After that there was no thought, just motion – and the most amazing sensation she'd ever experienced.

Chapter 19

"Houston, we have a problem."

Isabel's voice was accompanied by a gentle knock on the bathroom door.

"My name's not Houston," Eleanor shouted back from the bathtub where she was soaking her aching body.

Today's lesson had been gruelling. Having successfully achieved a few more bareback canters over the last few days - on the lunge line and then off, he'd let her progress to using a saddle now. This afternoon had only been the second time with full tack and she wasn't sure whether she didn't like it much because she missed the warmth of Blue's back and the directness of the connection or because she had been struggling to learn to rise to the trot. Pike had been merciless. There had been a point when she had wondered whether being a riding instructor required having a seriously cruel streak, around about the time when he had asked her to cross the stirrups over in front of the saddle and rise purely from the power of her calf muscles rather than push herself up with her feet. Now every bit of flesh below her waist felt like it was on fire.

Isabel tried the door handle. Eleanor sighed, got out of the bath and, leaving a trail of foam and water on the floor, hobbled to turn the key before scurrying back into the tub. Isabel opened the door, grinning.

"No but I nearly did call you Whitney."

"I think that would have been what they generally call a near miss. – Do come in."

"Can I sit down?"

"I'm not sure, try it," Eleanor grinned.

Since Isabel had consented to Eleanor's ponyfication, as she called it, their relationship had been stronger than ever, cemented with almost constant banter flying around the house.

Isabel gently let down her colossal mass on the toilet seat. The baby was due to be delivered by Caesarian in a couple of days, much to Isabel's frustration who didn't like the idea of an unnatural birth but who had conceded that it was wiser not to put any unnecessary strain on the tiny boy's heart. With all the extra ultrasounds it had been impossible to keep his gender concealed, so they knew for certain that it would be a boy – although they still didn't know what, if anything, was wrong with his heart. Interestingly, even with the big day drawing nearer, it remained Isabel who took everything in her stride, telling everyone that heart murmurs in babies were quite a common phenomenon, while Kjell, despite his medical background, was constantly fretting.

Eleanor for her part generally tried not to think about it. Not because she didn't care but because the whole concept of being a sister still seemed utterly alien to her, whether it be to a healthy or not so healthy baby.

Looking across to her mum now, who was absentmindedly staring down at her belly and stroking it lightly, she felt almost guilty for not...*err*....*participating?*

She was still searching for a better word, when Isabel took a deep breath, prompting Eleanor to sit up in the tub, exposing her breasts.

She glanced down at them.

She was sure they had grown. A little.

When she looked back up, she found Isabel looking at them, too, a half frown on her forehead.

"Your body's changing, Elle."

"Hm. - I believe that's what's supposed to happen, mum."

"Not just your breasts, all of you. You're getting hips and thighs and a bum. – You're not sleeping with him, are you?"

"What!?" Eleanor hid her face in her hands and rubbed her eyes, then peeked through her fingers, shaking her head.

"I was just thinking. I was flat as a pancake until I met your dad."

Eleanor let herself slide down, looking up at the ceiling. With her ears submerged in the lukewarm water her voice sounded deeper to herself, more throaty, when she answered.

"Yeah, mum, look, I know biology wasn't your strongest subject, so let me explain this to you. It's the hormones that change your body and make you want to go and have sex. It's not sex that makes you have hormones and form a body."

She came back up to grin at her mum.

"Hm," Isabel didn't laugh and carried on undeterred, "but if you *were* to sleep with him…"

"MUM!"

"…you'd take precautions, right?"

Eleanor sighed.

"Yes, mum, aside from the fact that I'm *fourteen* and probably a midget and this scrawny body of mine is still not even *thinking* of starting a period, if I was ever to sleep with Peter Pike of all people, you can bet your bottom it would involve probably a triple layer of condoms. Their whole house is full of them. Did you not see that? They come as standard in the guest rooms, right next to the tea tray. Have you *met* his parents? *I* have. They work in AIDS research. They're totally obsessed. They talk about nothing else. Pike reckons he never even had real balloons for his birthday parties as a kid," she stopped herself there, suddenly acutely aware that she wasn't exactly helping allay her mum's fears, "and like I said before: it's not that kind of thing. We are *friends* mum. Not even that, I think I'm kind of like a pet to him. Like a pet project, you know. Sometimes I get the feeling he's just using me to prove something. I don't know what, but I'm pretty sure he'll lose interest as soon as Blue goes."

There you go, I've said it. Stab myself in the chest a few more times, why don't I?

"Hm," Isabel smiled at her knowingly, "I don't think so. – Anyway…"

"Yes, anyway," Eleanor interrupted, "where are you going with this? What's the problem?"

"The problem is that mum just rang. She can't come to look after you while we're in hospital because she's in hospital herself, as we speak, with a broken foot. The silly woman was putting her suitcase in the car this morning and apparently it slipped and fell on her foot. And because she was wearing sandals and the suitcase is metal - and probably contained a kettle, an iron and a dishwasher - all the bones in her right foot got squished. It's probably going to need operating on."

"Oh."

"Oh indeed. - So as far as I can see we've got three options. I can put you on a plane to Sydney at the bargain bucket price of about three grand, you can go and stay at Jon's," she paused, shut her eyes and took a deep breath, "*or* we can ask whether there's room for you at Hawthorne Cottage."

"Wow," Eleanor was astonished, "I don't want to go to Sydney and be so far away from you," she shrugged, "I could be at Jon's. - What would you prefer?"

Isabel pulled a face.

"That's the funny thing. I think I'd feel most relaxed if you were with Peter and Aaron."

She'd met the old man on Eleanor's birthday when she'd taken her daughter to the cottage to officially give her permission to ride and had instantly liked him. There was something tender in the way she asked Eleanor every time she came back from the cottage, how Aaron was, that made Eleanor suspect the special fondness was rooted somewhere in Isabel's loss of her own father early in life. Since their initial meeting, whenever one of her pregnant woman's nesting frenzies had expressed itself in a bake-a-thon or cooking-to-feed-the-5000 she'd given an embarrassed Eleanor a share in the results to take to the Cottage. Nevertheless, Eleanor was surprised at her choice.

"I'm confused. A minute ago, it sounded like you wouldn't trust us."

"Oh no - no, no, no, no," Isabel heaved herself up, grinning at her daughter, "I absolutely trust Peter. I just don't trust *you*."

Chapter 20

Two days later, in the small hours of a Thursday morning in late August, Eleanor got out of Kjell's car, kissed her mother goodbye, wished them good luck and let a bleary eyed Pike take her bag from the boot.

The night temperature had dropped over the last week, announcing an early autumn, and the cold morning breeze coupled with worry, nerves and anticipation made Eleanor shiver violently under the thin summer coat she'd thrown on over her pyjamas.

As Kjell turned the car around outside Hawthorne Cottage, Pike slung an arm around her shoulders from behind and pulled her into his bathrobe. From the warmth and safety of this sudden, unexpected shelter, she waved them off.

They remained like this long after the car had disappeared on the horizon, staring into the distance, neither wanting to leave the huddled position they'd assumed. He wrapped his other arm around her as well and drew her backwards into a proper hug, curling around her like a child around a teddy bear.

Eleanor closed her eyes and let herself fall for a moment. It was the first physical contact they'd shared since the day he'd marched her home - aside from his hands adjusting various bits of her body when on the pony – and Eleanor could easily have stayed in his embrace forever.

"What time's the op?" he asked quietly above her head.

"I don't know. They've got to check in at 7am, then they get told. They wait with the schedule until they know what emergencies there are. Kjell will text me."

They still hadn't moved. He buried his face in her hair and took a deep breath.

"Hm. You smell of cherries. You scared?"

Depends on what we're talking about here.

"Terrified. - That'll be the cake she baked for the nurses last night."

"Hm. Cake." He straightened up, grabbed her bag and took her hand. "Come milady, I shall show you to your room."

A short while later Eleanor found herself sitting on a comfy double bed in the yellow room on the second floor, swinging her legs and looking around. There were fresh towels in the en suite and a wall mounted TV. Her bag was resting on a desk, ready to be unpacked into an ancient sandalwood wardrobe that smelled faintly of lavender. Pike had left her some books on the bedside table.

"I didn't know what you like, so I picked out a bit of everything. You can always come up and choose something for yourself," he'd said before he'd disappeared downstairs. Eleanor had only been to his room once before, on her birthday, when he'd taken her and Isabel on the grand tour and showed them the view from up there, but the prevailing memory was that of books everywhere. On shelves, in neat piles on the floor, even lining the windy stairs going up. She looked through the selection he'd made for her. A book on horse care *(of course)*, "War Horse" *(read it)*, "Northern Lights" *(ditto)*, "Cat's Cradle" *(aha)*. She picked up the slender paperback and turned it in her hands, then opened it at random.

"Hey, how are you doing?" He'd reappeared in the door carrying mugs of tea. "Here," he put one down on the bedside table for her, "You can make your own any time you like, too," he nodded at the tea making tray on a small chest of drawers, "or just come down to the kitchen."

He looked at the book in her hand and smiled.

"Good choice."

He blew on his tea, took a sip then scanned the room a last time.

104

"Right. For what it's worth, I'm going back to bed. Anything you need, I'm only at the top of the stairs." He disappeared. She heard the corridor door to the watchtower fall shut and his muffled steps going up the stairs.

Suddenly Eleanor felt utterly alone.

Pike? Pike! - Please.

The sound stopped. There was a beat. Then the footsteps seemed to turn around and come back down slowly, hesitantly. Another beat, then the corridor door opened again and he appeared in the door frame.

He didn't smile or even look at her when he offered his hand.

Come.

They climbed the stairs in silence and soundlessly clambered into his bed. As she snuggled up against him and he lowered the duvet over her, drawing her into another spoon hug, he uttered just one word.

"Behave."

Then he gently kissed her, once, on the side of the neck - and although Eleanor thought it shouldn't have been possible to fall asleep when every cell of your being was tingling with electricity, she almost immediately slipped into unconsciousness.

It was nearly one o'clock when she woke with a start. Her phone was still in the yellow room and for all she knew all sorts of things had happened.

Their bodies were still more or less entangled in the same position they had fallen asleep in and she could feel his chest rise and fall rhythmically against her back as she listened to his long, deep breaths. She wriggled herself out of his embrace gently, so as not to wake him, then swung her legs out of bed and sat up.

Sunshine fell brightly through the bare window, directly onto a blown up photograph mounted opposite the bed. It was the only evidence in this room stuffed with books, console games and general boy clutter of Pike's interest in horses. It showed a tri-coloured mare, the kind that would be ridden by an Indian Chief in an early Western, with her foal – a carbon copy of her colouring - at foot. They'd been caught mid-canter, running with a herd, the mare's mane flowing in the wind and the foal's long legs all a tangle. It was an impressive shot and once Eleanor had got up and navigated her way across the mess on the floor to look out of the window at a solitary Blue dozing sullenly in the paddock, she wasn't at all surprised that for a moment she could see a vision of the little grey mare running happily next to the one in the picture.

Pike was right, she needed to be with her own kind - and soon. Eleanor sighed then left the room and the sleeping boy to find her phone.

The message told her that she hadn't missed anything. The Caesarian had been scheduled for 3pm to ensure a paediatric heart specialist could be on stand by, just in case. Eleanor didn't like the sound of it one bit but without any power to do anything, she tried not to think about it. She needed company. She got dressed and went down into the kitchen, where she found Aaron at the table solving a sudoku.

"Good afternoon, young lady," he smiled raising a mug to his lips, "Any news?"

"Nothing yet. Delivery is at 3pm. So that they can have a heart surgeon for the baby there as well. I don't like it." She sat down heavily on the chair Aaron had pulled out for her. He put his hand on the back of hers and gave it a reassuring squeeze.

"Don't worry. They're in one of the finest hospitals in the country and as far as I understand it, they haven't managed to find anything wrong with your little brother's heart as yet. Chances are he'll be absolutely fine. They're just being very cautious, that's all. And that's a good thing. – Now, where's Peter? He should be cooking you breakfast."

"I'm fine. I'm not hungry. I can't eat when I'm nervous. He's still asleep."

Aaron looked at her with no comprehension in his eyes. She might as well have said 'he's wrestling a baby panda'.

"He is *what?*"

"Asleep."

When he spoke again it was very quietly and with the kind of tremor in his voice that happens when old people swallow back tears.

"How long? - How long has he been asleep for?"

"I don't know. - It was probably six, half six?"

As the old man glanced at the clock, a single tear ran down his cheek. He looked back at Eleanor and squeezed her hand again, this time with gratitude.

"Thank you."

Eleanor never got a chance to ask what for because just then the boy in question appeared in the kitchen.

"Right," he yawned, "breakfasts all around, yeah?"

The news came in the early evening, first in form of a picture message showing an exhausted but smiley Isabel with a crumpled baby in her arms, followed shortly by a phone call from an elated, relieved Kjell. It looked like although little Oscar did have a congenital heart defect it was a comparatively minor affair, a hole in the heart so small it would in all likelihood close itself as he grew and that wouldn't need surgery or prevent them from coming home in a couple of days or so.

When Kjell finished the call, Eleanor let herself fall backwards onto the grass with a scream of relief and looked up into the blue sky. They had been sitting around in the paddock all day, Eleanor feeling unable to be caged inside or to do anything other than just be - and Pike keeping her company while oscillating between pulling ragwort and attempting to play the guitar. Blue was hiding from the racket he was making as far away as possible and now that she felt free to hear again, Eleanor could not fault the pony. Playing the guitar truly was something Peter Pike was awful at.

"I take it all is well then," he enquired while looking down, trying to get his grubby fingers around a certain chord – although, when Eleanor lifted her head up and looked at the arrangement of his digits she couldn't for the life of her figure out, *which* chord that might be. He was practically reinventing playing the instrument altogether. She sat up.

"Yep. All is well. Isn't it amazing, all this drama for nothing. – I should teach you, you know. I might not be the greatest guitar player in the world but I am his daughter, so I guess you could do worse," she hesitated for a moment then added more quietly, "could be our thing when Blue is gone."

He looked up, fixing her with his eyes. There was respect in them for her matter-of-factness about the mare's looming departure but also something else. Something so grand and...*unfeasible*, it made her heart stop.

"I don't think we'll need a thing, do you?" he asked under his breath.

She held his gaze for a moment, watching the mahogany specks do their flickering dance in the sea of amber. Icy fear started spreading through her veins but she decided to ignore it, grinning widely instead.

"No," she jumped to her feet, "But you, my friend, desperately need to learn to play."

And then she ran.

Chapter 21

Eleanor woke early the next morning, once more snugly cocooned in Pike's embrace. Even with the threat of devastation lifted, there hadn't been any question about the sleeping arrangements. This was where she belonged and it had remained innocent enough.

Her mum had only been half right: although there were parts of Eleanor crying out for way more than just cuddling together and a singular kiss on the neck, which he had repeated the evening before with the same word attached, there was an equally large part of her that simply wasn't ready.

One day, she thought and felt the tingling in her stomach as she imagined what it would be like to kiss him. She'd snogged a boy she hadn't even known in a bathroom at a party in Gloucester, about a year ago, to see what it was like and it had been good.

Very good.

And it had left her wondering what it would be like with someone who actually mattered to you. Since then, she'd fantasised about sex a lot but in that same hazy way that as a little girl she'd dreamed about meeting the tree spirits at the end of the garden, who'd whisk her away to *her* land, her true home.

Since she'd met Pike, the fantasies had become a lot more solid, a lot more real, a lot more *active* - although she remained careful not to think about him directly.

Presently, engulfed in his scent, with his arm lightly resting on her waist and his face buried in her hair that proved exceedingly difficult though.

She pressed her legs together and held her breath for a moment.

"Stop it," he mumbled sleepily, rolling his lower half to lie on his front without moving the rest.

She felt herself blush.

"Stop what?"

"You know what."

"Why?"

"Because I'm only human, Eleanor."

She turned around to face him but he kept his eyes closed.
"And?"

"And I don't want to spoil this. *Please,*" he opened his eyes, looking at her imploringly, "I haven't slept more than a couple of hours a night in *two years*, Eleanor. Now you're here, suddenly I sleep. Let me sleep. Don't ruin it. - Sex ruins everything."

She looked at him aghast.

"What do you mean you haven't slept in two years?"

He hesitated, then took a deep breath.

"PTSD - Post traumatic stress disorder. Does that mean anything to you?"

Eleanor nodded.

"Vaguely."

She lifted her hand to gently trace some of the scars on his face with her finger.

"From the accident," she stated matter-of-factly.

He sighed.

"Who told you about it?"

"No one. Your grandfather mentioned it once or twice but didn't tell me anything. And I overheard Tinkerbelle say something at school. Said you were two sandwiches short of a picnic since the crash."

He sighed.

"She's a bitch and a turncoat but she's not a liar. - She's right. I am. I'm on medication, Eleanor - and I see a therapist once a week."

He had retracted into a foetal position and shut his eyes again, almost as if he was bracing himself for her to leave. Eleanor took his hand and weaved her fingers through his. Even her summer tanned skin seemed bright white against the reddish brown of his. She stroked the side of his index finger with her thumb, her heart beating wildly.

"Does it help?"

"What? The therapy?"

"Yeah."

"She's very good," he opened his eyes again, smiling, "She told me to go and catch the pixie I saw in my paddock."

"Sprite," Eleanor corrected, smiling back at him, "Clever woman."

She hesitated then dropped her voice.

"Will you tell me about it?"

"What? The accident?"

Eleanor nodded and watched him swallow hard. He disentangled his fingers from hers and cupped her cheek in his hand, his thumb resting lightly on her nose. He gently pulled her in to lay his forehead against hers.

"One day. I promise," he drew back, "But not today. Today should be about celebrating life, not wallowing in death. What time are you going to meet your brother?"

"Kjell is coming to pick me up at two."

"Perfect. So we'll go for a nice morning ride out."

Eleanor felt almost dizzy with the sudden change of step.

"What? Out out?"

"Yep. Out out. Proper little hack. And I don't want to hear that you are not ready. You are and I'll walk with you. – Up you get."

And with that he pushed her out of bed.

A while later as she rode out of the twitten onto the open land and looked across the seemingly never-ending fields in front of her, she realised what he'd meant. When he'd said, 'what riding is really about', when he'd said 'about celebrating life' and when he'd said 'because the pony you're with is happy to be alive and alive with you'.

She enjoyed every minute she spend with Blue and loved both the mind link with the animal and the technical aspects of schooling because they were all about chain reactions between her body and the body of the mare and because this was the first physical skill she'd encountered other than swimming where her size simply didn't matter – but out here it was something else.

Given the choice she had opted to go bareback today and she could feel every inch of pony muscle underneath her fill with joy as Blue looked around, alert, snorting happily, ready for adventure.

Eleanor leant forward slightly as they went up the gently sloping bridleway to the top of the nearest hill.

"And that's what I mean," Pike said, walking next to her, "You're a natural. You're instincts are spot on. I didn't even tell you that. But, yeah, lean forward when you go up and backward when you go down."

"It's obvious," she beamed at him.

"Is it?" he asked mockingly, "Well then, I'm sure it's also obvious that you are meant to trot or canter up to the top." He winked at her.

"What?"

"You heard, up you go. Stick to the grass. Keep it nice and soft for her. We -"

"- don't trot on hard ground. *I know.*"

"Off you go then, little Miss Know-it-all. Wait at that big bush just before you get to the top. By all means let her graze until I catch up with you."

"What if I can't stop her?"

"Rubbish."

"What if she bolts with me?"

"I'd be very surprised - but if she does, you rip her into a very tight circle, or cling on and let her run herself out."

"What if she bucks?"

"Highly unlikely. You'll come off and it'll probably hurt. Try and roll away from the feet."

112

"What if I slide off?"

"Don't be daft. It's not that steep a hill. – Now stop fretting, pull in your tummy muscles, give her a squeeze and off you go. You know the aids."

Eleanor's body was so used to following his commands that the next minute she found herself trotting up the path without any more hesitation. She felt wobbly at first, having to negotiate the new element of inclining her body but after a short while she managed to hook her pelvic bone in behind Blue's shoulders and off they went in a steady trot line. The rhythm was different out here. While in the schooling paddock the well trained pony would automatically take her nose down and arch her neck high in what was called 'going in an outline', out here her nose was well in front of her, her eyes firmly on the horizon. Nevertheless, Eleanor felt herself getting ready and the pony underneath responded as soon as she felt the girl change position.

The canter was fast and exhilarating and Eleanor found herself quite breathless and somewhat relieved to be able to rein the little mare to a halt, when she got to the bush he'd pointed out. She turned the pony around, so she could watch Pike approach, let go of the reins and scratched the animal's back, just behind her own bottom. This was the signal for Blue that she was allowed to graze and after the longest of happy snorts she put her nose down and started ripping at the long grass greedily. Despite having all the paddocks of Hawthorne Cottage to herself, the grass out here somehow seemed to taste a million times better. With the mare settled into munching, Eleanor looked down the path, beaming at Pike.

She was still so elated by what she'd just done, it took her a moment to realise that something was wrong, off kilter. Then it hit her: he hadn't moved. He hadn't been catching up with her but had stopped where she'd left him, looking up at her from afar.

For a moment her eyes seemed to play a trick on her and he appeared almost transparent against the green.

When the flashes of comprehension came, they came in rapid succession as her blood ran hot and cold and the pulse of naked horror started beating behind her ears.

You wanted to prove to me that I could do this without you.

You're planning on leaving.

Soon.

Forever.

Suddenly Blue ripped up her head, spun around and gave a loud whinny, leaving Eleanor fully occupied with staying on and shortening up the reins and with no more time to dwell on what she had just foreseen. In the distance she heard another horse's voice answer the mare back and underneath her it felt like the pony had suddenly shrunk a couple of inches lengthways as all the muscles tensed up in anticipation.

A group of four riders were coming over the brow of the hill and down the path towards them, led by a massive bay horse. The rider's legs barely made it past the saddle flaps but she sat relaxed, her face turned to the side as she was chatting to the girl riding a chestnut pony by her right flank. Eleanor recognised Tinkerbelle long before the girl turned her attention back to the way ahead and spotted Eleanor. The other two riders in the group were riding to her left with one trying desperately to control a small pony, no taller than Blue and of a similarly odd grey, only gingery rather than bluish. It was prancing, head held high and calling to Blue who was standing to attention, answering back. Eleanor had never before felt like just a passenger on the little mare's back but now she felt like the pony had entirely forgotten she was there.

Surplus to requirement.

Eleanor saw Tinkerbelle clock her, stop the bay, turn to the girl on the red roan, say something and then veer off to the right, off the path onto the open green. The other riders followed her as she went parallel to the top, first into a trot and then a canter, away from Eleanor and Blue.

Eleanor instantaneously knew she had lost.

As she tugged her cheek into her collar bone and braced herself for rolling, she heard a loud whistle midair. She hit the ground hard and fast, rolling a couple of times before ending up somehow sitting on her haunches. When she looked up she saw Blue stopping mid-gallop, half way to where the other horses had sped off, looking backwards and forwards between Pike and the horizon where her friend had disappeared. Pike whistled again and she turned, head hanging low and started walking back towards him and Eleanor. Pike who'd come running up the path got to Eleanor just before the pony did, out of breath and pale. Blue arrived looking confusedly at her rider on the ground.

'What are you doing down there?'

Pike knelt down in front of Eleanor and held her by the shoulders.

"Are you alright? That bloody cow. She knows better than that. She knew Blue would try and run after Strawberry. I'm so sorry, Eleanor. Are you hurt? You roll well. I don't even think you need a new hat."

Her shoulder, the first point of impact, burned like hell but she knew instinctively that it wasn't broken. She looked at him, shaking, tears streaming down her face.

"I'm alright," she shoved him angrily, "but you're not. - You total bastard."

She scrambled to her feet, grabbed Blue's reins, pushed the mare into a ditch, shakily jumped back on her off jelly legs and turned her home.

He came after her.

"Hey, I said I'm sorry. I wasn't to know, they would turn up, was I?"

She reined the pony to a halt, waited for him to reach their side then turned to look straight at him through tears of anger.

"I'm not talking about that. That was just her being a bitch. – I…I *saw*, Peter."

Through her shaking voice it came out all wrong, as if 'Peter' had no 'r' in it yet an extra 'a' here or there and she didn't know whether he flinched because of how it made his name, a name she'd never before called him by, sound or because he knew.

His only saving grace was that he didn't deny it.

Chapter 22

She didn't feel remotely alright again until the moment she gingerly picked up her baby brother to hold him close. She breathed in deeply, taking in his newborn smell, while he was trying to suckle on her neck.

Eleanor wasn't what she called a 'babies' girl' - someone who would go all gooey over puppies, kittens, babies and all things miniature and who would have known what they wanted to call their children from the age of about four – but as she hugged the little boy, a wave of love went through her that washed away all the anger and grief she'd been carrying with her since the morning. All she was left with was a primeval desire to shield and protect this small human from all harm. She unstuck him gently from her neck with a finger and held him, so she could see into his eyes.

"Hello, Oscar. Nice to meet you. Glad you made it," she kissed him on the forehead and handed him back to Isabel, "Here, I think he's hungry."

Isabel beamed at her, took the baby and put him on a breast. Once he was securely latched on and drinking greedily, she looked back at Eleanor, searching her face. "How are *you,* hon? How is it going at Hawthorne Cottage?"

Terribly, thanks for asking. I now know that the one person in the universe who can look straight into my soul is planning on killing himself at some point soon. I've felt better but hey-hum.

"Alright." Eleanor was trying to sound casual. "But I think I want to sleep at home tonight. Is Kjell still staying here or is he going back to the house?"

Isabel looked tired, her complexion was cheesy and pale, with huge rings under her puffed up eyes - but even exhausted and post-Caesarian, there was no hope in hell, she wasn't going to pick up on Eleanor's state. The only question was whether she was going to pull her up on it or not.

She cocked her head and studied her daughter through lowered eyelids for what seemed like an eternity. Finally, Eleanor could feel the mind probe retracting.

She's going to let it go. Good.

"Actually, we were discussing it earlier and I think Kjell was planning on going home, do some shopping, get things ready. He'll fetch us in the morning. So, yes, no problem. He might appreciate some help. – Oh, did I tell you that one of my midwives knew Peter's great-grandmother? Actually, she was trained by her. She was a midwife here."

Too easy. I should have known.

"Small world."

"They are a really interesting family."

"Hm."

I don't want to talk about him.

Isabel sighed, then gave up the game.

"Eleanor? What's up? What's happened. - Has he hurt you?"

No, but he is planning to. In a fairly permanent fashion.

"No. - Don't worry mum. He has been….the perfect gentleman. I just need –" she didn't know how to put it.

" – some head space?" her mum offered.

Eleanor nodded.

"I guess."

When she returned to Hawthorne Cottage to collect her things, he wasn't in the house.

Aaron, like her mum, obviously knew that something had happened between them but unlike Isabel, he didn't ask. Instead, he furnished Kjell with a cup of coffee while Eleanor went to gather her belongings, asking him all about the baby's birth. For a brief moment, as she was ascending the stairs to the watchtower, Eleanor

contemplated telling the old man what she'd seen but felt
bound by some absurd loyalty to the boy.

When she entered his room she hastily picked up her jeans
from the floor, the only remnant of her presence in here
over the last two nights. She didn't want to stay any longer
than necessary. She raced back down to the yellow room,
throwing everything into her bag, which had never got
unpacked into the wardrobe, closed it and went to find the
men in the kitchen.

They were sitting in silence, Aaron smoking a roll up
while Kjell was bent over some documents on the table in
front of him, making acknowledging noises as he read.
When Eleanor appeared in the door frame he looked up at
Aaron.

"Looks pretty straight forward. Do you mind if I take
these?"

"By all means. I'd appreciate it," the old man replied.
Kjell shoved the papers neatly into a manila envelope then
nodded at Eleanor. Now, that she was about to leave, she
felt terrible towards the old man who had shown her
nothing but kindness and who she was about to leave in
the dark about what she knew. She thanked him for his
hospitality and bade him goodbye with a hug. Kjell,
watchful yet quiet as ever, got up and took the bag from
her.

"I'm assuming you want to say goodbye to your pony. I'll
meet you by the car."

Eleanor nodded and went through the back door.

His bike was in the garden.

You're around. Where are you?

She went through the gate and down the twitten, heart
beating in her throat.

When she got to the metal gate, she saw him in the
paddock, pulling ragwort and throwing it on top of a
mountain of the poisonous weed, already heaped in a
wheel barrow. Blue was grazing nearby, constantly

keeping the same few feet distance from him wherever he moved. She looked up to greet Eleanor with a low nicker but didn't come over to her like she normally would have. Pike carried on regardless, ignoring her presence. Eleanor climbed the gate and sat on top, watching him for a moment.

How can you even think about it? Why???

"Here is what I don't understand," she heard herself say loudly, firmly, all the anger back in an instant, "why, if you're losing the land anyway and why, if you're going to throw it all away, are you still bothering with that? Blue is clever, she eats around it."

Upon hearing her name, the mare left his side for a moment and ambled over to Eleanor to lightly nuzzle her legs then rub her face gently up against her. Eleanor gave her a light scratch behind the ear.

I'll be back tomorrow. And every day until you leave. I promise.

Satisfied, the pony returned to grazing close to the boy. The challenge was still hanging in the air.

Finally he looked up, his eyes burning bright. He hesitated a moment before he walked over to stand in front of Eleanor, bringing with him a sickening smell, a cloud of the yellow poison. He took off the gardening gloves and grabbed the metal rail left and right of her bottom, bringing his face up to hers.

"That's what a custodian does, stupid. As long as I am the keeper of this land, I'll look after it. - I will still be pulling ragwort on the morning of the day Karen comes and the deeds are handed over. Then I'll put my gloves down. No sooner, no later."

"And then what? – A noose? A gun? An overdose? What? How? Go on, tell me."

"Actually, I was thinking Beachy Head."

"On the bike? Cheesy. But, hey, each to their own."

He was barely an inch away from her face now.

120

"Why are you so angry?"

She took a deep breath.

"Are you kidding me? - Because that wasn't the deal. – Because I don't want a ghost, thank you very much. Some people might think it's romantic. I don't. I've seen the reality of it. My nan's got one, my dad's mum. Has had him since she was, I don't know, younger than me. Her best friend. Died of a ruptured appendix. She *loved* that boy – and nobody will ever come close. My granddad, he will do anything for that woman but it's never good enough. And it never will be. Cause he's not him. You get it, *stupid*? You may be gone but the people who love you will still be here."

She'd stopped ranting now, tears welling up in her eyes again. "Why? I mean, really, seriously, why?"

"Why not?" it came back dryly.

"What?"

"Why not." His jaw was set now. "We all die. We're here and then we're gone. It's a foregone conclusion. And I can't be asked to wait around for the credits to roll, understand? So why the fuck not?"

She lifted his left hand from the bar, let it drop, turned and jumped off onto the twitten side. Suddenly much shorter than him again and with the gate between them, she felt dwarfed and helpless, all the fuel of anger having evaporated into pure despair.

"Like I said, the people who love you will still be here," she repeated under her breath, before adding defiantly, "and I refuse to be one of them. – I'm leaving. I'll see you tomorrow. Or not. Whatever. I'm going home. I'll be back for Blue every day. Until she goes."

Then she turned and walked away.

Chapter 23

Eleanor had never spent any length of time in Kjell's presence on her own before and it took her a while to figure out the right word to describe it.

Soothing, it suddenly crossed her mind somewhere between the cheese aisle and the frozen vegetables. His company was like a cool breeze on a hot summer's day or a mug of hot chocolate on a cold winter's night.

A leveller, she thought as she was watching him read yet another ingredients list, this time on a packet of peas, *it's like he rolls out the universe into a nice soft comfortable blanket to wrap around you.*

"Contains peas," he stated dead-pan as the packet landed in the trolley.

He was also remarkable funny but in a subtle way that you had to be prepared to find amusing. He didn't make you laugh, he invited you to laugh. Mostly about himself and all his idiosyncrasies, which he seemed to be acutely aware of, but also about all the little funny scenarios around, which he would point out with a surreptitious nod and a twinkle in his eye. A dog, mesmerised by a packet of sausages clearly visible through the thin plastic of its owner's shopping bag. A little girl, having an intense conversation with two oranges she was holding.

Eleanor knew that under normal circumstances she would have thoroughly enjoyed this little shopping trip; that she would have jumped at the chance to get to know him a bit better on their own terms, to develop their own patter, without Isabel's omnipresent interference - and that he would have had her in stitches by now.

Very gentle ones, but stitches nevertheless.

As it was, she felt too numb to barely manage a smile in response to his numerous, gentle attempts at bringing her out of her shell. In a hazy sort of way she felt guilty about it, too, because while not pushing it he wouldn't give up either.

Presently he was looking down into the trolley in despair, running a hand through his hair and shaking his head.

"I haven't got a clue what I'm doing. Look at it."

Eleanor did.

The peas. Lettuce. Every type of fruit imaginable. Nappies. Wipes. Juice. Eight different types of cheese. A giant packet of cream crackers. Coffee. Ovaltine. Bread. Milk. Butter. Olives. Sundried tomatoes. Anchovies. Capers. A salami ring.

"It'll make a good after dinner party with nibbles and a fruit salad," Eleanor offered.

"Hm. – I'm supposed to be doing a weekly shop. For a family. What do I know about shopping for a family? - Help."

For a moment Eleanor wasn't sure whether the mild panic was feigned for comedy value or real. Sometimes the accent, slight though it was, made it doubly hard to tell. She decided for the latter.

"Right," she said authoritatively, "forget about it. Oscar doesn't eat anyway and mum will need food to eat with one hand. That's what she always says is the worst thing about having a baby. You end up having to eat with one hand and people insist on giving you stuff you absolutely need both a knife and fork for. So, here's what I suggest: we get this stuff, it's all good stuff, maybe add some eggs and bacon and Marmite. Then we get out of here. When she comes home tomorrow we order one-handed food. And then she can tell us what she wants for the next few days and we'll go again. Agreed?"

"Agreed," he sighed, "Thank you, Eleanor."

It was starting to get dark by the time they arrived back home.

Standing in the kitchen, putting the last bits of shopping away, Kjell took a moment to contemplate the contents of the fridge before he shut the door resolutely and turned to Eleanor who'd just finished finding a home for the cream crackers.

"Right," he said, "how about the Italian on the beach? The one with the squid spaghetti and the home made ice cream?"

"Pardon?" Eleanor had been on auto pilot again. Lost in numbness, trying to push Pike further and further from her mind and soul, knowing she was failing miserably on one level yet at the same time winning way too easily on another.

After all, she was a pro.

One of the advantages of moving a lot at an early age was that you learned to like and lose on a regular basis. Maybe not to the extent that was required of her right now but practice made perfect. Already she was managing not to feel anything when she said his name in her head. She could remain cold while conjuring up his face as long as she focused on a neutral expression. Occasionally she would slip and see him flash that chipped toothed smile, the one that came with the dancing flames of joy in the sea of amber - and her heart would duly scream in pain. But then again, it had only been a few hours. Cutting anyone from your existence took a while, detaching from the first person you ever even contemplated to love would surely take a bit longer.

"Eleanor, are you alright?"

"What? Yeah. Sorry. I don't think I'm hungry."

"You're crying."

"What?"

Kjell was offering her a roll of kitchen towel from across the table where he was standing and suddenly Eleanor noticed that tears were streaming down her face. She tried to wipe them away with the back of her hand but realised there was too much water. She took the kitchen towel, ripped off a couple of sheets and wiped her face before blowing her nose. Every blow resonated in her sore shoulder and she winced. Snuffling back the remaining tears, she made a dismissive gesture.

"I'm fine. Just a bit emotional. Don't mind me."

Kjell drew a chair back from the table and sat down, looking at her through worried eyes.

"If it's about the pony…." he breathed out heavily, "We could ask them to sell her to us, you know. There are other stables around. I'm sure we can find a nice livery yard somewhere close. And we can afford to keep a pony, Eleanor. It doesn't need to end in a couple of weeks, you know."

She looked at him astonished.

For an instant, it seemed like the perfect way out.

They could stay together, Blue and her. And him. Maybe. If she could convince him.

She felt the hollowness of the solution follow only a second later. It wouldn't be the same. And she was fairly sure it wouldn't change his mind, on the contrary, something in the image of proposing the idea to him rang a whole belfry full of warning bells. It would make it worse, somehow. She wasn't quite sure how or why but she knew it would - something to do with desertion and rats leaving the sinking ship.

Why should it matter though? said a cold voice inside her head, *When he is gone, he's gone. What difference would it make? What's with this stupid loyalty thing?*

"Eleanor?"

Kjell's voice once again jerked her back into the room. She looked up and locked onto his grey green eyes, full of…*care,* she thought. *He really, actually cares.*

She slowly shook her head.

"It's not about the pony?"

She could feel tears welling up in her eyes again.

"It's about the boy," he stated flatly.

She began nodding then stopped herself.

Kjell blew out his cheeks, looked down at his hands and raised his eyebrows.

"That's a much taller order."

There was a moment of silence between them and then he stood up abruptly, went around the table and offered her a hand.

"Come on," he smiled reassuringly, "as a very good friend of my grandfather's used to say: there is hardly a problem without a solution. We'll figure something out. - Come out to eat with me and celebrate my second evening as a father."

She had nowhere else to be.

She slipped her palm into his and felt a cloak of neatly patted out blanket of infinity fold around her.

Maybe, just maybe, things would turn out alright.

At least for now she was going to believe that.

Her stomach grumbled loudly and Kjell laughed.

"Not hungry, eh? Come on, let's go eat some food."

Chapter 24

It was a beautiful, still but cool late summer's night. The tide was in and the sea lay dark and flat in front of them, just across the promenade and a strip of pebble beach away.

It had been well past dinner time when they'd arrived and they had managed to get one of the three highly coveted tables outside. From here you could see the throngs of people strolling along the seafront and watch the occasional queue of ice cream customers build up outside the place. It was famous beyond the borders of the town, a somewhat glamorised Gelateria that also served some decent pasta and seafood dishes.

Eleanor swallowed the last forkful of spaghetti marinara and looked across at Kjell who had finished his calamari a few minutes earlier and had pushed the plate aside in order to do some calculations in biro on a paper napkin.

"Pistachio," Eleanor stated, "Pistachio and Raspberry Ripple."

Kjell looked up from the napkin and across to the ice cream counter, where an elderly couple was choosing their cones. They had been watching them approach for a while, meandering along the promenade, kicking a stone along between them, giggling like teenagers.

"No way. I'd say she is After Eight and he is firmly Vanilla."

They'd been playing the game all evening.

"No," Eleanor said, "I meant me. - I think you might be right about them. They're cute aren't they? – What are you doing?"

"Calculating the future. – How long do you think they've been together?"

Eleanor contemplated them for a moment. Visually, there was nothing special about them - a thoroughly non-descript duo of humans in their sixties, of average looks, average heights and unspectacular clothing - yet the air between them seemed somehow denser than the air around them.

"Hard to tell," she shrugged, "the force is strong between them. They're definitely the love of each other's life, very…" she made a ball gesture between her hands, "…together. Very much a unit. - Possibly a duprass even." Kjell snorted a surprised laugh.

"You read Vonnegut?"

"I'm trying," she replied, feeling a knife twist in her stomach, all interest in ice cream seeping out of the gaping hole.

Damn. And we were doing so well.

"Impressive."

He looked at the couple again who were taking their cones now and turning away from the counter. They were coming towards them and just as they were about to pass the table, the man stopped, leant down and looked from Kjell to Eleanor and back.

"Lemon sorbet," he grinned, "I can't stand Vanilla." Then he followed his woman, putting an arm around her waist when he reached her, drawing her close as they walked back into the night.

Kjell watched them disappear and sighed.

"How do you rate my chances?"

"With mum? Getting that far? – Hm."

"That bad?"

Eleanor shrugged.

"I don't know. I mean you'll never…"

"…be Jerry," he finished the sentence for her and she nodded.

"I know. That's ok. Most of us have a Jerry. My Jerry is called Maria. We only put the North Sea between us rather than all the seven oceans like your parents but the principle is the same," he paused, staring into his wine glass, "Very few Isabels and Jerrys and Kjells and Marias make it, you know," he took a sip, "They burn out."

"Why?"

"Too much, too young. - You end up devouring each other whole if you're not careful. And then that thing, what you saw between those two," he tilted his head into the night, "it implodes and it becomes a burden. It's gone but because it was so grand you are always looking for it. - The ones who make it, are the ones that don't let that happen."

"How?"

He shrugged, finished his wine.

"If I knew that," he winked at her, smiling broadly now, "we wouldn't be sitting here and I wouldn't have a baby son with the most wonderful woman in the world and you wouldn't have a half Swedish baby brother. You can have more than one love of your life - and your mum is definitely one of mine."

There was a sadness behind the smile that spoke of his doubts as to whether it went both ways. He beckoned the waiter through the window.

Eleanor wanted to give him something back, for the sense of normality he'd wrapped around her tonight.

"I don't know," she said firmly, "but I think you stand a pretty good chance. - She's different with you. You're very different from the others. And you have a baby together."

Kjell beamed at her proudly.

"We do, don't we?"

It was in the taxi, half way home that she finally mustered the nerve to ask him.

It was a proper city cab type and she was sitting opposite him, with her back to the driver, looking out of the window at the lights going past. She'd always liked travelling backwards, looking at what she was leaving behind rather than what was coming up ahead, leaving the future shrouded in mystery. Her mum had often joked that she was made for life in a limousine.

"Kjell?"

"Hm?" He was tapping some buttons on his phone.

"What was in the brown envelope you took from Pike's house?"

"The loan agreement," he answered absentmindedly.

"What loan agreement?"

Kjell looked up at her, frowning.

"Has Peter not told you why they are losing the land?"

Eleanor shook her head. It had always been a given, something for which there was no reason as such, just an unchangeable fact.

"His aunt borrowed a lot of money, and I mean *a lot* of money, from this man who asked for the land as collateral. She can't pay it back, so the land becomes his at the end of this month."

"How much?"

Kjell named a sum that left Eleanor with eyebrows raised and puffed out cheeks.

She let the air go with a pop and took a deep breath.

"Wow. – Wonder what she borrowed it for?"

"Aaron says they did up the house with it. The roof, the whole building was in a really bad state and she had it all done. And then she had the en suites put in, so that they could rent out rooms. The contract was to pay it back within two years but I can't figure out how she thought she was going to make it back that quickly. It's not possible. She would have had to have rented out all rooms at top guesthouse rate all year round, just to pay the loan back. That's unrealistic to say the least. That's not even including running costs or their living expenses," he shook his head, "I don't think she really thought the terms of the loan through. The business plan was sound, just the time

130

scale impossible. You'd be looking at somewhere around a ten year payback period, minimum."

"Is the land really worth that much?"

Kjell shook his head.

"Not quite, no. Not as it is. Although land prices around here are so high, it's pretty close. But if you got planning permission for it, it would be worth a lot more. There is a housing shortage down here and land is scarce…"

A chill went through Eleanor and for the first time she truly understood the magnitude of what was being lost. It wasn't that the land was to become some*one* else's but possibly some*thing* else. She imagined standing in the watchtower and looking out onto houses or, worse, a block of flats instead of being able to see across paddocks and onto the next county.

She thought for a moment.

"Can't they borrow the money against the house? Like a mortgage or something? Hawthorne Cottage must be worth a fortune."

Kjell shook his head doubtfully.

"You have to pay a mortgage back and they are what you call asset rich and cash poor. Aaron hasn't got an income, neither has Peter. I don't know what his aunt earns now but it can't be much and I get the distinct feeling that Peter's father wouldn't allow the house to be put in jeopardy. From what Aaron tells me, it sounds like he is a traditionalist. Hawthorne Cottage has been in the family for over three hundred years. The land only came with Peter's great-great-grandmother. Her husband bought it for his wife, so she could keep her horses on it. And anything to do with the house, they all have to agree, whereas the land was left solely to Peter's aunt to be passed to him in the event of her death."

Eleanor looked at him in amazement.

"How do you know all this?"

He laughed and held up his phone, pointing at it in the pose of a housewife in an old ad for washing up liquid. "Suspend your disbelief and behold this object of wonder – it's called a telephone. Old people use it to spy on young people and share their worries."

"Oh," Eleanor didn't really know what to say.

Kjell winked at her then looked thoughtfully out of the window as they turned the corner into their road. He shook his head lightly.

"If that was my family, I wouldn't let it happen but between you and me, not that I have met him, Peter's father sounds like a bit of a prat."

Eleanor jerked in surprise. She'd never heard Kjell swear or judge another human being in any way before, let alone so negatively.

Interestingly, he was right.

The one time over the summer when Pike's parents had graced the cottage with their presence for a few hours had been an odd, stifled affair. If Eleanor hadn't known beforehand what relation they truly were to Pike and Aaron, she would have thought they were some distant relatives, second cousins twice removed or some such, on a courtesy visit.

Pike's mother, a wispy blonde woman called Alice with fair skin, pale blue eyes and a mantle of righteousness that she kept around her like a buffer to any real emotion, had been so indifferent towards her own son, it had been painful to watch. Coming away that day Eleanor had appreciated the often overbearing but always warm, vibrant and *loving* mother the universe had bestowed upon her more than ever before.

Pike's father, tall like Aaron, with dark, almost black eyes and the same broad facial features as his son, had moved in a cloud of unquestioned education and authority. Every inch the genius researcher. A true Hawthorne, as he had pointed out on various occasions during the day, which -

as he had informed Eleanor at great length - meant to be a doctor or at the very least a midwife or a nurse. Unlike his wife, Dr John Hawthorne – who had actually gone to the length of changing his name to match his ancestry by deed poll - obviously did have feelings for both his father and son. Mostly of the embarrassed and disappointed variety. As cold and superior as the two doctors had been towards the people surrounding them, as passionate they had been between themselves, endlessly talking about their research while casting a critical eye around the house and garden and lecturing 'the children' about the importance of safer sex. It had been a bizarre combination, the stuck up overly British-ness coupled with a factual, no-beating-about-the-bush attitude towards sexually transmitted diseases. After they had left, it had felt as if they had sucked all the energy out of the house. That night had been another one of those when Eleanor hadn't heard the little Yamaha return for a long, long time. She shuddered, thinking about it now, casting her mind back to earlier in the day, seeing Pike's set jaw, telling her he wasn't going to wait for the credits to roll.

How close had he come already? Was *his* righteousness about looking after the land really going to last long enough for her to make him *see*? She hoped so.

A defeated smile crept across her face as the taxi pulled up to the house and one of the longest days of her life was slowly coming to an end.

I might have said I was leaving but it's not like I get a choice. Hang on in there.

There was reconciliation in that thought and for a moment, as she was getting out of the cab, she truly believed that there would be a solution, that they could somehow make it, that he would come around and truly rejoin the living.

That's when she saw the guitar.

Chapter 25

When Eleanor walked through damp, heavy air towards the barn the next morning, she was exhausted to the point of rainbow flutters drifting across her retina.

Sleep had been a sporadic affair.

Despite trying everything not to think about it, she had lain awake all night, staring at the outline of his guitar resting against her wall in the semi-darkness, repeating their last conversation over and over in her head, feeling her heart wanting to break.

Please don't, please don't, please don't.

Round and round like a mantra.

Whenever she had managed to slip away into slumber, she had woken minutes later, either from pains in her shoulder or from bad dreams or both.

In one nightmare she'd seen him drowning, not in the sea but in a dark river and she was there, holding on to him, fighting the current that was trying to drag him away but ultimately losing the battle, just as he said he wanted to live. Then it changed and she herself was the one drowning – before waking up, gasping for air.

Please don't. Just don't.

In another, they were running away, up the beach and across the paddocks, fleeing from a tsunami like wave, which got him and dragged him away as he shouted at her to run and not stop.

Stay. Just stay.

In yet another, they were on a boat, happy, laughing – until they realised their feet were getting wet. They were sinking fast and he put a life vest on her before diving under deck to free his horse. Next thing, she was floating in the water, with the tri-coloured mare from the photograph swimming alongside her. And in the dream the horse could talk and told her he hadn't made it.

Please.

When she had woken from the last one, some time around dawn, the pains in her shoulder had got company from cramps in her pelvic region and when she'd gone to the toilet, she'd realised with a start that she'd started spotting blood. She'd wedged one of her mum's sanitary towels, much too bulky for her, in her pants and had got dressed. Then she had sat in the kitchen for a couple of hours, staring into space, feeling around the ether for his presence, almost sure he hadn't left this plane of existence yet but wishing she was still at Hawthorne Cottage, wishing to know for certain that he was safe, that he'd been serious about not putting his gloves down yet, that leaving the guitar had just been a...*a what?*

At the break of dawn, when the synapses in her brain had started twisting back on themselves, just after she'd tried to ring his dead phone for the hundredth time, she'd ended up dialling her father's number instead and had got the answer she'd expected, served with a raspy laugh.

Then she'd stared into space again - until Kjell had got up and given her a lift.

She had made a promise to Blue and she was going to keep it, whatever the outcome.

The mist hung low over the land and she wasn't surprised when she crossed the paddocks not to find the pony out and about. One thing she had learned about the little mare was that she preferred milling around in the barn when the air was humid. Her heart sank, though, when she got to the stables and couldn't see her anywhere. Maybe she had been picked up already? Maybe Pike's aunt had come last night? She wasn't supposed to yet, but maybe...?

Suddenly her blood ran cold.

What if her feeling was wrong?

What if he *was* gone and he'd taken Blue with him?

He wouldn't do that. I can still feel them. Close.

Just then, she heard a commotion and laughter from the tack room.

When she got to the door she found the pony standing in the middle of the room, watching over Pike, laid out on the sofa. Each time he tried to move the mare would shuffle, push him back with her nose gently and not let him get up. When Eleanor appeared in the door frame, Blue turned around and looked at her, blowing out a long snort.

'About time, too.'

She let off Pike and ambled over, rubbing her forehead gently against the girl's chest before moving out into the stable area, leaving her humans behind in search of food.

"What was that?" Eleanor asked evenly, relief washing over her.

"A trick gone wrong," he answered dryly.

For half an eternity they seemed suspended in time and space.

Now that she was here and he was still alive, all she wanted to do was to hold him until he would change his mind. But what good would it do? She couldn't hold on to him forever. She wished he would understand. How precious life was, how his argument against it was actually every argument *for* it.

We live, we die. But we need to live life first. With all the pleasure and pain it offers. Otherwise we can't die.

Eleanor knew that with every fibre of her existence, knew it with every note she'd ever sung, every chord she'd ever played, with every moment she'd spent on Blue's back, every moment she'd spent in his company - and she wanted him to know it, too. But she also knew she couldn't force him.

Suddenly she felt a nudge in her back.

And then another.

Blue had returned and was gently pushing her along, towards him.

He smiled then clicked his fingers three times. The pony sighed and retreated.

"Pike…" Eleanor started but she didn't know what to say and her voice trailed off. She stood there, head hanging, arms limply by her side, feeling tired and helpless and broken. She focused on a speck of dirt on the floor, let herself fall through it and for a moment knew that tomorrow she would wake up an old woman, looking back on this day, this moment, wondering where her life had gone. But it would be alright – if he was by her side. Finally, she raised her head.

"I don't want you to die," she said lamely, "not yet anyway."

He grinned widely.

"That sounds like one day you might just want me to." He jumped up from the sofa, came towards her, grabbed her by the waist and lifted her up to eye level. She automatically slung her arms and legs around him and there she sat, suspended on his arms now, which he'd crossed under her bottom. He looked at her, the amber in his eyes almost completely absorbed by the mahogany fire but not in anger or pain, but love.

"You're an amazing person, Eleanor, and you have an amazing gift. But you need to learn to be a bit more patient with the rest of us."

He took a few steps backward and sat back on the sofa, still holding her tight.

"Who is this 'us'?" she asked, raising an eyebrow, leaning back on his lap.

"Me," he sighed, resting his forehead against her chest, talking down, "You have to be more patient with me. I'm…I've never felt like this about a person. Only… about…a horse. - And then I heard her die. A slow, horrific death." He looked up at Eleanor again, tears in his eyes. "She wasn't like Blue. Blue is my friend and my teacher, like a big sister, you know. People think I've trained her well. You know her now, you'll get what I mean when I say she's trained me well. – Inara, that was something else. She was my everything. You know, *my* horse, my soul mate. She was my last thought at night and my first thought in the morning…" his voice trailed off before he steeled himself again, "and then she was gone and my world fell apart. People say I'm crazy because she was just a horse and that Karen and I got lucky - but you know, part of me died that day. And I've felt out of synch ever since. It's like I've been walking next to myself for the last two years. - Then you turn up. And at first I thought you were like a, I don't know, like a last project, something to leave behind, you know. Someone to pass some of my skills to, before I…" he shrugged.

"And now?" Eleanor asked quietly.

"I don't know. All I know is that when you said yesterday that you refused to be one of the people who loved me, it hurt. Like hell. And I know that although Inara is still the first thing I think of in the morning, she isn't the last thing I think of at night anymore. - And that feels good but also wrong…I don't know…disloyal, I guess."

He was leaning against her chest again, the last sentence having been mumbled somewhere between her still barely existing breasts.

Looking down on his head, she ran her fingers through his hair.

"So what now?"

"I don't know," he looked up and shrugged, "I thought maybe you *could* teach me to play the guitar."

"That's why you left it outside my house?"

"That's why I left it outside your house."

They both knew it was a lie and they both knew neither of them was ever going to change that story.

"It will take a long, long time," Eleanor grinned, "you're absolutely awful."

"Doesn't matter. We've got all the time in the world."

Eleanor could feel her chest expand, finally being able to breathe freely again.

"Promise?"

"Promise."

"Come hell or high water?"

"Come hell or high water." He sniggered at the outdated expression.

"Good," she stated, "But not today. I'm too tired, I haven't slept all night."

"Me neither."

"Hm. – Sleep with me?"

He smiled, the hint of a smirk appearing around the corners of his mouth.

One day.

She clipped him around the ear.

"You know what I meant."

Chapter 26

"Give her all the reins, work her over the back more. Keep giving her little squeezes. Not so she hurries but so she steps under and engages the hind. She is supposed to stretch down with her nose just above the ground, not slouch around looking for food while pretending to work. If you are doing it right, you can feel her back arch towards you."

Eleanor was trying hard but the watchers were seriously interfering with her concentration and ability to connect. Her face was already hot and sweaty despite this just being the warm up to the lesson.

Where had they all come from?

It had been most peculiar, as if with Pike's decision to stay on this side of eternity for the time being an invisibility cloak had been lifted from the land.

The whole of the summer the three of them – Blue, him and herself – had been pottering along on their own. Nobody had shown any interest, visitors had not got further than Hawthorne Cottage, not even a dog walker or curious child had ever peeked across the gate. Now, in the last few days, it seemed like the place was heaving.

Every day someone or other had turned up.

On the first one, an old livery of Karen's had ridden up to the gate, oblivious to the state of affairs and had asked whether there was room at the inn for a horse and a pony, only to learn to her obvious shock that the inn was no more.

The following morning, Pike's father had suddenly appeared in the barn as part of an unannounced visit to Hawthorne Cottage. It had been a very strange affair, which had seemed almost scripted to Eleanor. Like father and son were following some ancient ritual that had survived the turn of the tides, fashions, morals and attitudes since time began.

It had started with him laying into the boy about school and about 'snapping out of it', to which Pike had retorted that it was the summer holidays.

The next round had revolved around the need to keep up the Hawthorne family's tradition to have a doctor in every generation, at which point Pike had suggested sarcastically that in that case, John and Alice had better get some IVF and produce another baby, or maybe adopt an African one to train appropriately.

In the last round, John had gone into a long rant about the foolishness of horse people and as a final blow had delivered a below-the-belt line about Karen's debt. Pike had coldly pointed out that if his parents had looked up from their research occasionally to see what was going on around them, they would have found that the very house that went with the very tradition John was so proud of had had the roof cave in on itself - and that it had been Karen who'd put her livelihood on the line for the cottage and not the fine doctors.

By this point, father and son had ended up eye-balling each other, faces only inches apart and for a moment Eleanor had seriously expected some form of violence to erupt. Instead, they'd held each other's gaze and after what felt like hours, John had finally backed down, sighed, taken a step backwards, put a hand on his son's shoulder and nodded ever so slightly before turning to leave.

Then he had walked over to Eleanor, examining her long and hard before telling her he hoped she knew what she was letting herself in for and wishing her good luck. When he'd disappeared again, Eleanor had sought Pike's eyes, afraid the encounter would have him waver but all she'd met was astonishment and resolve.

In the end they'd shrugged it off and had gone about their day, learning from Aaron later that Pike's parents had left for a three month research trip to South Africa that afternoon. It saddened Eleanor that his mum had not even come in to say goodbye. She could feel herself getting upset about it again now but pulled herself together when she sensed Blue becoming increasingly annoyed with her. *You're right, sorry, I'm not focusing.*

She felt the pony almost nod in agreement underneath her. This was only her second ride since the fall. The day before, when her shoulder had felt good enough, they had gone out, up the twitten and around a field just in walk and trot with Pike staying firmly by her side this time, jogging along.

On the way back a couple of little girls, out for a walk with their mum and dog, had attached themselves to them and had asked a million and one questions about ponies in general and Blue in specific, before cheekily begging for a ride once they had followed them all the way back to the gate.

To Eleanor's surprise, Pike had not fobbed them off but had invited them in. Then, with the mum's permission, both girls had been given the same kind of taster lesson in the schooling paddock Eleanor had been treated to on her first day. It had been an odd sensation, watching him do with them what he had done with her. She had felt a twinge of jealousy when she'd seen the second girl's face – the first one hadn't been so keen once the reality of a sentient, breathing being underneath her had hit home – break into that same delighted smile Eleanor knew she had worn back then. Part of her wished she could go back to that moment, the same way she often wished when she'd read a good book that she could erase it from her memory and read it again for the first time.

But that hadn't been all of it.

She'd realised she didn't like the idea of others riding *her* pony, which was, she suspected, what had got her today's audience. She had confided her feelings to Kjell when she'd got home, slightly embarrassed of the childish possessiveness but knowing he would understand. He'd reassured her and, in between changing a nappy, had requested to see her ride.

Eleanor hadn't realised that he'd meant 'tomorrow' and had been somewhat thrown off kilter when they had turned up at the yard that morning – Kjell, Isabel, Oscar and even Aaron – deck chairs at the ready. Pike had frowned at the intrusion but after muttering a disapproving 'deck chairs!' under his breath had made them feel as welcome as possible, paying particular attention to Isabel who felt clearly out of her comfort zone around Blue but was trying hard not to show it.

The ice had broken somewhat when the mare had respectfully looked into the sling, in which Oscar was asleep, head resting sideways on a breast, and had flared her nostrils only to very gently blow some warm air in his face. This had elicited a happy smile on the sleeping boy's face and had reassured Isabel enough to lift a hand and hesitantly touch the pony's soft nose, stating 'She is very gentle, isn't she?'.

It was then that the nature of the visit had dawned on Eleanor.

She hadn't told Pike about Kjell's suggestion to buy Blue, neither had she ever really told Kjell what she thought of the idea and suddenly she had felt incredibly awkward. She hadn't been given the opportunity to set the record straight there and then either because everything had been in motion and there didn't seem to be an opening: while Aaron had set up the chairs and had settled Isabel and Oscar in, Kjell had told her to tack up, asking Pike to show him the grounds and the stables in the meantime. Eleanor had got the pony ready absentmindedly, biting her lip and wondering what to do.

She wanted to keep Blue, badly.

The idea of her being carted off to the other side of the country wrenched at her heart strings. But more than anything she didn't want to hurt Pike. What she really wanted, she sighed to herself as she was tightening the girth straps, was for everything to stay as it was. For the land to be saved, for Blue to stay and get a companion, maybe one Pike could ride - just like she'd suggested so naively on that morning he'd marched her back home, aeons ago.

When he'd come back from giving Kjell the tour she had started saying something but he had tersely told her 'later', then helped her with the girth and disappeared to the other side of the pony to hold the right stirrup for her while mounting.

"Eleanor, turn in at A and halt at X, please," Pike's voice reeled her back into the present.

She did as she was told, still on a long rein and steering solely with her weight and legs, picking up the reins only for the halt. Pike stepped up to her, put a hand on her thigh and looked at her searchingly.

"Are you alright? You're not concentrating at all. Is your shoulder hurting? Or is it just them? Are you nervous?"

"Very. I - "

"Don't be," he interrupted, "You're already light years ahead of where you should be. Kjell will see that. He is a horse person. And judging by the questions he just asked me while we were going around, I'd guess a pretty good one. He'll know how long it takes to learn to ride and he knows you've only just started. Relax."

As he said it, Eleanor realised that Kjell was probably the one person she wasn't worried about in this scenario and it occurred to her that the same couldn't be said for Pike. There was a need for approval here, a desire for the older man to recognise the work they had done.

"I'll be alright. Don't worry," she nodded at him reassuringly.

"I'll take it from here," Kjell's voice suddenly sounded across from the deck chairs as he got up and made to enter the schooling area.

Eleanor and Pike looked at him aghast.

"What?" It came out as one voice.

Kjell approached, smiling broadly.

"I'll take it from here," he repeated as he arrived in the middle of the school.

"I want to see what you can do, Eleanor, and I happen to know that horses tend to tune into a familiar instructor rather than the rider if need be. And they predict what the instructor will ask next based on knowing that person's patterns. We all have them. But she doesn't know me, so she will have to tune into you alone, which is what I want to see. So I'll take it from here. - You don't mind, do you?"

The question was aimed at Pike and he put up his hands, gesturing 'all yours'.

"So what can she do?" Kjell asked the boy.

"She can walk, trot and canter bareback and she can rise to the trot in the saddle but when she canters with a saddle she still finds it easier to flip the stirrups over and still holds on to the pommel for the transition."

'She' is just here, Eleanor desperately wanted to interject, feeling a bit like a car or motorbike or, indeed, a horse being appraised but she bit her tongue.

Kjell made an approving sound, then nodded to Pike to leave the arena.

"Ok, time to pick up the reins, off you go at walk towards C, left hand rein please…"

He took over seamlessly.

Chapter 27

Eleanor had to admit afterwards that she had got a lot out of Kjell's lesson.

He had been right, Pike had figures he favoured and often she could predict what he would request next. This was even truer for Blue who'd known the boy all his life. Having to follow the commands of an entirely different instructor doubled their concentration and effort. Any thoughts outside of the task at hand were kept firmly at bay by straining to fulfil whatever was expected.

And Kjell's expectations were high, it transpired quickly. He asked everything he had been told they could do and then some, such as a halt from trot, which they had never done before, or keeping the stirrups down in canter, which led to Eleanor promptly losing one. He didn't let off until both girl and pony were out of puff, sweaty and tired, then helped Eleanor take the saddle off and gave her a leg back up to cool the pony down bareback on a long rein.

He patted Blue's neck, flashed Eleanor a big smile and with a 'you'll find us in the cottage kitchen when you're done' left them to get on with it.

Only then did Eleanor realise that Isabel, Oscar and Aaron had vanished from the sidelines and just Pike had remained, beaming at her proudly.

As Kjell passed him on the way out, there was a brief exchange between the two that Eleanor couldn't hear but seeing the expression on the boy's face and the spring in his step when he came towards her, she didn't need the details.

She'd never seen him happier.

He gave her a bear hug while she was still sitting on the pony.

"You were brilliant. Thank you, Eleanor. And you," he patted Blue's neck and slipped her a treat from his pocket.

"Your work," Eleanor mumbled shyly and started biting her lip again.

He narrowed his eyes and looked at her inquisitively.

"Alright. Out with it. What's bothering you?"

She was looking at her hands when she replied, at the reins sitting in her loose fists so naturally.

"I think...I think Kjell wants to buy Blue from you. For me," she added unnecessarily.

There was a sharp intake of breath before he replied.

"That's not gonna happen, Eleanor, I'm sorry," he looked up into her eyes, which were welling up with tears and swallowed hard, "I...I don't want to hurt you. You're the last person on earth I ever want to see hurt but when this here," he gestured around, "is finished, she deserves, she *needs* to go home. - And home for a horse is where her herd is. And what little is left of her herd, Strawberry aside, is up in Scotland. If she was younger, you'd be the only person in the world I would be happy to give her to but she's twenty-five, Eleanor. Yes, she's a native and yes, she might with luck and care have another ten years left in her but she owes us nothing and we, I, owe her everything. She's been through so much in the last couple of years and when this land, the land she was born on, is gone I want her to be with her herd - and with Karen. Sorry."

Eleanor was nodding through the tears, trying to let him know she understood. She tried a smile.

"But I get to keep you, right?"

"Yep. You absolutely get to keep me."

"Good." She breathed out heavily and leant forward to hug the neck of the pony, burying her face in the mane for a few moments, then slid off.

"I'm ready."

As it happened, there had been no need to brace herself for turning down one of the kindest offers anyone could ever make.

Once they had joined the others in the cottage kitchen for the delicious traditional roast Aaron had conjured up, no word was lost around the idea of buying Blue and when Pike mentioned probingly that Karen was coming at the weekend to pick her up, the only reaction was from Isabel - to invite them all to a gig on the Friday. Ebony, whose album had made it into the mainstream charts, was coming to play one of the mid-sized venues in town and had requested for them to be her guests.

Boy and girl looked at each other across the table to share a shrug and a smile. They'd obviously got it wrong.

But it would be good, they thought in unison, to have something that would take their minds off the inevitable the night before. They toasted to Ebony's success and leant back into the cosy comfort of a meal shared with family and friends, taking turns in cradling Oscar, so Isabel could have a civilised meal eaten with knife and fork.

After pudding, Isabel retired with the baby to the sitting room for a feed and when Aaron also disappeared to make a phone call, Eleanor and Pike found themselves alone at the table with a thoughtful Kjell sitting between them at the long side of the L-shaped bench, stirring his coffee. There was a sobriety surrounding him that didn't allow for anything but the most truthful answers, once he began questioning them.

"I need to know something from you two," he began but left it hanging for a moment before continuing, "Do you think you could still be friends even when you're not together anymore?"

"We're...we're not together now," Eleanor stated.

Pike narrowed his eyes and shot her an amused glance. "Aren't we?"

Eleanor could feel herself blush and looked down at her hands.

"Well, we're not...you know," she looked up again.

"Sleeping together? Yes we are. We're just not having sex," he said it bluntly, a rough, cut-the-crap edge to his voice, "and we're not going to for a long, long time if I can help it. - But neither," he added softly, still holding her gaze, "do I want you doing anyone else, if I'm honest."

She smiled back at him and for a second there were only the two of them in the room. Kjell, respectful as ever, let them have their moment before sombrely posing the next question.

"What if she did?" he fixed the boy.

Pike smiled sadly, defeatedly, as if it had already happened.

"Then I would have to accept that," the smile morphed into a grin, "It wouldn't change that she is in my karass though. So either way, I'll get to keep her on some level. That's going to have to be good enough, I guess."

A flicker of recognition passed over Kjell's face.

"Good answer. - Right," he turned to Eleanor, "what about you?"

"What about me?"

"If Peter went to sleep with someone else, would you still be able to be friends with him?"

"Depends. - Before or after?"

"Pardon?" Kjell looked dumbfounded.

Eleanor grinned widely.

"Well. If he goes and sleeps with someone *after* he's finally slept with me, fine. Bitter, but fine. If he goes and sleeps with someone else *before* ever sleeping with me," Eleanor looked away from Kjell and straight at Pike who seemed to know exactly what was coming for he had picked up a grape from cheese board and was poised to throw it at her, "I'll kill him."

It hit her on the forehead.

Kjell smiled warmly looking from one to the other, blew out his cheeks, took a sip from his coffee and stared into the mug for a while.

"How did I do?" Eleanor broke the silence.

"Pardon?"

"How did *I* do?"

Just then Aaron appeared in the door frame and gave Kjell a brief nod. Kjell nodded back then turned to Eleanor.

"Equally good answer," he said distractedly while getting up, "excuse me."

He left them, more puzzled than before.

"I got it," Pike suddenly mumbled into the nape of her neck as they lay in his bed later that night, "they *are* looking at buying a pony. Just not Blue. They're thinking about something we both can ride. I bet that's what that was all about. That's why my grandpa is implicated. The sly bastard."

"Language," Eleanor murmured.

Right now, she couldn't have cared less. She was half asleep, wrapped in his being and every one of his words had resonated against her skin to send shivers down her spine and through her core. She shuffled back, snuggling deeper into him. "Tell me more."

"Uh uh." He laughed quietly and kissed her neck.

"I know, I know," she sighed, "behave."

Chapter 28

Eleanor found herself mulling over what he'd said the night before while she was brushing Blue the next afternoon.

They were alone together. The morning had been a wash out and Pike, Eleanor and the guitar had spent it in bed until his fingers had hurt from practice and her ears had bled from patience. After lunch the rain had cleared off and he'd left on the Yamaha for a doctor's appointment, giving Eleanor and the pony a window of opportunity for some serious grooming time.

Eleanor could get lost in this task for hours.

She loved cleaning and massaging the little mare with the different brushes, loved scratching her with her fingernails in those places where nothing else would do, loved watching her zone out and fall into a trance, bottom lip flopping down loosely and the occasional contented shudder rippling through her body. She loved running her fingers through the coat against the direction it grew in to watch the hairs fall back into their original position like a black and white flick book; loved it when Blue would suddenly wake up from her reverie to gently start grooming her back, always knowing exactly not to pinch anything other than clothes with her teeth and using lips only on any exposed skin. Eleanor couldn't for the life of her imagine sharing the same tenderness with another pony.

Two days left.

She could feel herself well up at the thought.

Did she even want to carry on riding once Blue had gone? And where would they keep another pony? Could there really be an 'after Blue'?

Pike had told her about how people normally moved on from one pony to the next, bigger, one to eventually a horse and then a better horse and so on, as if they were a commodity rather than entities with a heart and soul. He had shown her how many for sale ads came with the tag 'sadly outgrown' and she had sensed his pride for being part of a family that would not, had never been forced to, do that. He'd also started telling her more about Karen, who at only eleven years old had helped drag Blueberry out of her mother and into the world and who, according to him, was the finest horse woman in the country. At least since the death of his grandma Kimi who had been the best British stunt rider of her time, working for travelling shows, on TV and in movies, until she'd met a young blacksmith called Aaron Pike and had taken him home to live at Hawthorne Cottage in order to pass her skills on to the next generations. Whenever Pike spoke of these women Eleanor would end up feeling immensely grateful to them, for their knowledge that was now coming her way but even more so because it was clearly their love for this boy that had kept his fire burning through a childhood of rejection by his parents. Eleanor still didn't know why Karen had left but everything she had heard about her by now made her feel almost ashamed of the anger she had once felt towards the unknown woman. Chances were, she had done whatever was best for her horses and – so Pike had finally told her – she had asked both Aaron and him to come to Scotland with her. It had been them who had refused to leave the house, the land and the past.

With that, Eleanor's thoughts were about to come full circle and return to the question whether she even wanted another pony after Blue had left, when the little mare suddenly ripped her head up and started dancing on her toes. Her ears were playing in all directions and she began whinnying in rapid succession at the top of her voice. Eleanor took an instinctive step back and swiftly pulled apart the panic knot she had tied her up with. Just then she could hear a horse answering from the direction of the gate and also a human voice calling faintly in the distance. "Excuse me? Hello? Anyone here? I think I need some help."

Eleanor started walking, taking Blue with her. The little mare appeared to become more collected, yet on another level more excited, with every step that brought them closer to the gate. As they approached, Eleanor could see an elderly lady in a dark pink riding hat steadying herself on the gate, straining against the long-maned, white horse she was leading and that was agitatedly prancing and neighing. The saddle hung askew from the side of the animal and the woman's face was ashen. She was resting the arm she wasn't using to hold on to the horse's reins across her chest but despite obviously being hurt kept control of the horse with what appeared to be sheer willpower.

"Hi there," she smiled weakly when she spotted Eleanor, "I think I might need some help. Is there…is there a grown up around?"

She was clearly starting to lose her strength and the fight against the animal but Eleanor realised that the horse was getting a little calmer as it saw Blue approach.

"We're as good as it gets right now, I'm afraid. Step back for a sec," Eleanor answered calmly.

She opened the gate, told Blue to back up and beckoned the woman and the horse in. As they walked through, horse and pony sniffed each other and there was a little squeal. Pike had once told her that this would normally signal the beginning of a scrap for dominance but as Eleanor witnessed it in reality for the first time, all she saw was two horses too happy to see another of their kind to pursue the ritual any further. She shut the gate and told the woman to follow her to the barn. Once inside, she tied up Blue again and went to take the horse's reins. It felt strange, having to handle a different horse, especially one

that was so much taller than Blue and so skittish, but
Eleanor didn't have much time to think or fret about it.
The woman who'd maintained silence looked as if she
was about to faint, so Eleanor told her to sit on an
upturned crate by the wall and got on with unsaddling the
horse. It proved difficult from this angle while still
holding the reins, making her fumble quite a lot before
finally succeeding. As soon as the wonky thing was off
the horse, however, it immediately relaxed a little. Eleanor
took the horse into Blue's stable, which was always made
up and left open for the little mare to come and go as she
pleased, took the bridle off, checked that there was water
in the bucket and then left it ripping hectically at some hay
in a net.

She shut the door firmly behind her and looked at the pale
rider hunched over on the crate, cradling her hurt arm.
"I'll be back in a tic, then we'll get you help," she said
softly before freeing Blue and putting her out into a
paddock. The pony followed her somewhat reluctantly,
clearly annoyed that the other horse had been put in her
stable and was not going to be running in the field with
her. As Eleanor closed off the fence, she saw Pike's
familiar stature approach across the fields. Relieved, she
flagged her arms at him but didn't wait for him to get
closer once it was clear he'd got the message. Instead, she
turned and hurried back to the woman, afraid she might
have blacked out by now.

She hadn't but neither had her skin tone improved. She
had stopped cradling herself, was resting her head against
the wall with her eyes shut and appeared to be doing some
form of breathing exercise, arm lying limply in her lap.
When she heard Eleanor approach she opened her eyes
and watched the girl crouch down in front of her.
"Have you called for help?"
"Not yet. I've only put your horse in the stable and put my
pony away."

154

The woman nodded in approval.

"Animals first. Quite so."

"But my friend is just coming. He lives opposite. He'll sort you out."

"I think my wrist is broken. - Could you help me take my hat off?"

"Sure." Eleanor gently released the clip under the lady's chin and took the helmet off. Once her head wasn't encased anymore it became clear that she was one of those lucky people who could only be described as a timeless beauty. Her short white hair accentuated a face that was perfectly proportioned, with a fine long nose, above which sat eyes of a dark blue, so near to black it bordered on the colour of an autumn night sky. Although she was probably in her sixties, her tanned skin was smooth with the exception of an abundance of laughter lines around the eyes and the corners of the mouth. Her still full lips went into a faint smile.

"You're very kind, child. What's your name?"

"Eleanor. - And this is Peter," Eleanor nodded in direction of Pike who'd just arrived at the barn door, taking in the scene while catching his breath.

"Hi there," the lady uttered visibly relieved at the arrival of the boy, "I'm Sarah. Pleased to meet you. I think I've broken my wrist."

"What happened?" He asked as he came towards them, stopping outside the occupied stable for the fraction of a second to take in the sudden addition. He whistled softly. "Pretty. She's an Andalusian, isn't she?"

The woman smiled at him as he arrived in front of her and knelt down to examine her injury.

"You know your horses, young man. Yes she is."

She winced as Pike gently lifted her arm and ran his fingers down the bone. Watching him, Eleanor couldn't help but think that he probably *would* make a good real Hawthorne if he wanted to, even more so when he began questioning his patient as to how it happened and whether she was hurt anywhere else.

"No, just my wrist," Sarah replied, "The saddle slipped and I slid off more than fell. But my foot got caught in the stirrups and in my panic that she would drag me, I started fumbling, freed my foot but twisted my hand. I could literally feel my wrist crack. - It's my own stupid fault," she continued, "I've got weak hands, you see. I can't really do the girth up properly anymore. Normally Robert, Robert Greaves up at The Black Horse, does it for me or the girl they have, Charly. She's very good, too. Very strong. But neither of them was available today so I let this other girl help me...and she obviously didn't do it up tight enough. We were fine for the first hour because we were taking it slowly but then as we were coming down that chalk path, I lost my balance a little and when the saddle slipped, Casta shied and that was that," she finished on a sharp intake of breath as Pike put her hand back down.

Eleanor had been watching from across the aisle where she was leaning against Blue's stable, stroking the white mare over the top of the door. She was breathtakingly beautiful but also quite highly strung, fidgeting in the strange stable between taking mouthfuls of hay. Eleanor was trying to soothe her nerves somewhat with long massaging strokes along the neck whenever she would stop long enough for it but it didn't seem to do much good. With one eye on the horse and one on Pike she couldn't be entirely sure but thought she could sense him tense up beyond the friendly, reassuring poker face he was showing Sarah.

"Right," he said standing up, "there is a first aid kit in the tack room. We're going to put your hand in a sling and then we're going to take you to the house and phone a cab to get you to the hospital."

Sarah's eyes followed him up as she nodded in agreement.

"Funny," she said, "You seem familiar. You really remind me of someone but I can't put my finger on it."

"I get that a lot," he answered evasively, already on his way to the tack room.

"How much is a cab to the hospital going to cost? I have no money on me," she called after him.

"About twenty quid. It's fine. We'll sort you out. Pay us back another time."

He'd disappeared into the tack room and Sarah sighed deeply, looking at Eleanor.

"Twenty Pounds. That's a lot."

It surprised Eleanor that a lady as fine looking as Sarah with a horse as stunning as Casta should be worried about twenty pounds. Sarah smiled sadly, picking up on the girl's thoughts.

"We're all glitter and no substance, her and me. To be frank, I haven't got two pennies to rub together. I've been working and living in Spain for the last twenty years. Managed a riding holiday complex. Turned seventy in April, got hoofed out. I was silly, I have no pension plan, nothing." She sighed again. "And I spent what little I did have saved to get Casta over here. She's got to earn her living now, poor soul. She's in working livery at The Black Horse. Oh god - " her face suddenly fell, "how am I going to get her back there? She's booked in for a one-to-one dressage lesson tomorrow morning. I can't afford for her not to do it. This is a nightmare. I'm going to have to ring Robert and get him to pick her up in the horsebox."

"He's going to charge you, if you do. Fifty at least, I'd say," Pike stated, returning with a bandage and a sling in his hands. He crouched down in front of her again.

"No?" Sarah's voice had that particular ring of a person simultaneously astonished yet not really surprised.

"Yes," Pike confirmed while expertly starting to bandage her wrist, "That's what you get for dealing with arseholes."

"Excuse me? - Now, listen young man, he might be a very tough business man but everything Robert Greaves does is well above board. Agreeing to the deal we have has helped me out tremendously, so I think that might be a bit strong."

Although Eleanor could only see the back of Pike's head she knew that his eyes had gone bright mahogany when he replied.

"You clearly haven't met him yet."

Chapter 29

"You!" Sarah exclaimed as they entered the kitchen and she saw Aaron sitting in his familiar place, reading the latest issue of National Geographic.

"Lady Sarah!" The old man seemed perplexed, almost shy, for a moment, then put out the roll up he was smoking, shuffled to his feet and came over to pull a chair out.

"Oh my word," she continued as she sat down looking around, "I did think the grounds and the house looked familiar. But I only came here the once, for your wedding reception and everything looked very different then. Where are your horses, where is Kimi?" she half made to get up again, "I must go and say hello."

Aaron gently pushed her back into the chair, looked into her eyes and ever so slightly shook his head.

"Kimi died, Sarah. Cancer took her."

Sarah's good hand came up to squeeze his arm.

"Oh no," tears shot into her eyes, "Oh god, I'm so sorry Aaron."

"It's alright. She's been gone a long time now. Eight years in November."

He said it reassuringly, soothingly, yet the hurt in his eyes betrayed his words. Eleanor had never heard the old man speak about his dead wife before but it became clear in an instant that she still owned his heart.

"So, what's happened to your arm then?" Aaron enquired, changing the subject swiftly.

Between them Sarah, Eleanor and Pike explained the chain of events before it was agreed, against some feeble protesting from Sarah, that Aaron would accompany her to the hospital. Sarah seemed grateful for being looked after yet was also still clearly uncomfortable with the idea of borrowing the cab fare, highlighting her financial situation once more.

"I honestly couldn't tell you when I can pay it back," she pointed out one last time before a taxi was finally called.

"Don't you worry about that," Aaron reassured her, "and where your horse is concerned, Peter can ride her back for you, can't you boy?"

Pike drew in a sharp breath, shooting daggers at his grandfather but when he saw Sarah's face light up, agreed nevertheless. Sarah's expression suddenly changed into a worried look.

"No offence but do you think you can handle her? She needs a very still rider. Someone with a properly independent seat. If you move too much she can get very agitated. Robert only uses her for the very best riders. She's very popular."

Pike's mouth broke into a sarcastic grin.

"I bet."

"Sarah?" Aaron caught her attention then added firmly, "He is Kimi's grandson. He can handle whatever horse you chuck at him."

"Of course," Sarah frowned looking at Pike, "I said you seemed familiar, didn't I? I'm never wrong about these things. I can see Kimimela in you and I can see you, too," she smiled in direction of Aaron then turned back to the boy, "I'm sure you'll be fine. But if possible do take Eleanor and the pony with you. Casta is much better in company and she doesn't know you."

And so it came that after two years, Peter Pike finally got back on a horse.

He held Eleanor's stirrup for her first, reeling off one instruction after another about riding in company. Eleanor could see the corner of his top lip vibrating.

"Nervous?" she asked.

"Very," he answered.

This was one of the many things she loved about this boy. There was no pretence with him, no bravado – at least not towards her. He could be difficult to be around, all emotions always being turned up a notch higher than with most people but with it came an honesty that made it all worthwhile.

"But you are Peter Pike," she said, gently mocking him as her foot fished for the stirrup.

"Uhu. But she's still a horse I've never ridden and a skittish one at that. My grandma used to say she never stopped getting butterflies with a new ride. – And I haven't been on one in a while, you know," he added with a wink, pushing her heel down, before leaving her side to untie the white mare and lead her across the fields and through the gate.

Eleanor and Blue followed them out and stood to the side, so he could shut it behind them. He was wearing Sarah's helmet and Casta kept sniffing at it nervously as if to reassure herself with the familiar scent hanging on the hat. Pike slowly pulled the stirrups down, adjusted them to his length by measuring them up against his arm then crossed the right one over in front of the pommel. As he put his foot in the other stirrup and gently slithered up along the saddle flap, he kept talking to the mare in a low voice, telling her how pretty she was, how she was going to enjoy their little ride home, how he was never going to force her to do anything and so on. His movements remained unhurried and measured, matching his words and before the horse knew it he had swung a leg over and – keeping his body low above the withers – was rotating himself to face the front before slowly edging up into a seated position. All the while he kept talking and stroking her neck. Once he was on, he took his left foot out of the stirrup and crossed this one over the withers, too. They stood for a moment and he breathed deeply a couple of times before letting the reins glide through his fingers and invisibly, silently asking her to move off. The mare responded and as she stretched her long neck, walking past Eleanor and Blue, breathed out a drawn out, happy snort. Pike gave Eleanor an almost imperceptible nod and she filtered in behind him, leaving a horse length distance. Together, they rode up the twitten.

They had gone far beyond the furthest point Eleanor had ever reached before, when he took both reins into his left and without turning signalled for Eleanor and Blue to ride up to his side. They adhered to his request at a light trot, slowing back to a walk when they found themselves two abreast.
"Hey," he said without taking his eyes off the horizon, "How are you doing? Keeping up alright?"
"Yes," answered Eleanor, "Blue doesn't seem to have any trouble."
"Good."
It was true, although the Spanish mare was three and half hands taller than the pony they seemed very well matched in speed. While Blue was a brisk walker out here, every stride aimed at covering as much ground as possible, Casta's gait was quite slow, deliberate and elegant. Eleanor stole a sideways glance and had to catch her breath as her heart did a somersault.
They looked stunning.
Despite the somewhat strange attire Pike was wearing - the fuchsia hat, which clashed violently with the colour of his skin, an army surplus shirt in fatigues' green, a pair of terracotta jodhpurs that had once belonged to Karen (a foot too short, baggy around the thighs and gathered in with a belt) and black combat boots – he cut an amazing figure on the horse. There was the elegance of a dancer in the way he sat, which incorporated everything he'd taught Eleanor and then some, and the mare stepped out accordingly, visibly enjoying having such a wonderful dancing partner.

Mental note, she thought blushing inwardly, *the ineptitude in guitar playing does not come from a lack in rhythm.*
He cocked his head and flashed her a smile.

"Up for a little trot?"

They had long got to the top of the chalk path and had veered off to the right along the brow of the hill. The view from up here was breathtaking, offering rolling hills to three sides and the ocean behind them. It made Eleanor feel giddy with joy. She nodded and he gently uncrossed the stirrups, lowered them down and slipped his feet in.

"Why did you do that?" Eleanor asked.

"Do what?"

"Mount like that. Like she had never been mounted before or something. I mean, if she is used for lessons, she must be used to it, right?"

He snorted a laugh.

"Habit. It's how my grandma would get on a horse she'd never ridden before if she had to ride with a saddle. It's what she taught us. It's gentler for the horse and safer for you. You fall clean and you roll better should they buck or jump or rear. – Also," his voice dropped taking on a dark tone, "I know how Robert works. Just because he uses her, doesn't mean she is used to it." He stroked the white horse's neck. "And I want her to enjoy being ridden by me." There was a sad smile on his face now and he swallowed hard. "How about that trot now?"

Eleanor responded by asking Blue with a light squeeze and off they went.

He kept pace next to her, starting to rise to it at first but after a few minutes just sitting it out, riding one-handed and smiling broadly. When they slowed back to a walk after a while he was laughing, patting his horse's neck.

"Man, she's comfortable to sit! What a dream!"

Casta seemed to echo his joy, giving a few long snorts until Blue, too, joined in.

Eleanor beamed back at him.

"So," she called across, heart beating fast, "where's the canter stretch along here then?"

He reined Casta back to a halt and waited for Eleanor to follow suit, then rode up and turned the white mare a quarter to face girl and pony sideways.

"Are you sure? You don't need to do this for me, you know. And I don't want you hitting the deck again." Eleanor smiled.

But I do, she thought, *I do have to do this for you.*

"Don't worry, I won't," she said.

And she didn't.

Just.

There was a hairy moment when Blue suddenly seemed to change into a long, flat bullet, picking up enormous speed. The canter became uncomfortable to sit and Eleanor had to hold on to the pommel, leaning forward into the wind and clinging on with all her might. But before long there was that familiar whistle from Pike who had kept Casta back to make sure Eleanor wasn't getting left face down in the dirt without him noticing. Blue immediately slowed down to a steadier rhythm and eventually Eleanor felt secure enough to let go of the saddle again, regaining control to rein the pony back in, first to a trot and finally a walk.

She could hear him laughing as they approached from behind - a joyous, elated laugh like she'd never heard from him before. When they appeared by her side it was at some strange gait, like a trot in slow motion with Casta flinging her forelegs high in front of her and every step suspended in midair for a fraction of a second.

"What's that?" Eleanor exclaimed.

"For one of her, a bit of a sloppy Passage...for an Olympian Warmblood probably a ten out of ten," he chuckled then released Casta into a normal trot for a second before slowing her down to a walk. "It's weird," he added more quietly after a while, "she rides a lot like Inara. You can really tell the American Indian Horse came from Spanish horses. Even with five centuries in between. How strange is that..."

After that, they rode next to one another in silence for a while.

"You need to learn to stand up in the stirrups for the gallop, Eleanor," he said thoughtfully after a few minutes, "You can sit it out low above the withers when you're bareback because your centre of balance is lower above the horse. But if you have the extra height of a saddle between you, you've got to stand up, shift the balance into your legs. That was dodgy back then."

"And when do I learn that?" Eleanor asked.

"Normally, I'd say there is no time like the present," he said looking across and shaking his head, "but she's already quite sweaty and starting to flag. And we still got a way to go. I'm wondering whether it was such a good idea to bring her. She's fitter than she was before you turned up but she is still not *that* fit and..."

"...she's twenty-five," Eleanor finished the sentence for him, "Do you reckon I should get off and just lead her for a bit?"

Pike turned his head and smiled at her warmly.

"Not yet, but you might just have to walk home on your own feet with the rest of us."

Eleanor shrugged, patting her pony's sweaty neck.

"So be it."

Chapter 30

It had never occurred to Eleanor that even in the horse world there could be different types of clean and tidy until they silently rode up past the imposing sign announcing their entry into The Black Horse Equestrian Centre. Whereas the first time she had seen Hawthorne Barn its spotlessness had screamed desertion at her, the immaculately kept grounds of The Black Horse that flanked a driveway framed by meticulously weeded flower beds advertised a busy but tightly run ship, where every blade of grass knew its place.

It felt stifling and as they came closer to the imposing main building, to the right of which was a sand school of Olympic dimensions, Eleanor wasn't surprised that every one of the gaggle of girls who were watching a lesson from the fence was dressed in beige jodhpurs and expensive boots.

As they rode into the yard a shiny silver horsebox that looked as if it had just left a dealership's showroom passed them on its way out. She was surprised to see Pike, who'd become increasingly tense and introverted as they had neared their destination, smile and wave at the driver with genuine warmth. She didn't get to think about it more, though, as one of the girls turned to take a look at the new arrivals, whereupon a screech escaped her lips.

"Oh my god. It's Peter! Everyone look, it's Peter."

She jumped off the fence and all five of them left their position to come over, chattering animatedly as they approached. When they had reached half way, Pike cut through the increasing noise level.

"Ladies, tone it down and stop there please, let me get off first."

They did as they were told and Eleanor caught a glimpse of Tinkerbelle on her Warmblood in the school, shooting an annoyed glance in their general direction. She did a double take but then collected herself, focusing again on her instructor, a grey-haired woman with a harsh voice who seemed oblivious to anything else going on. Pike had swung himself out of the saddle, put the stirrups up and was presently loosening Casta's girth. He gestured to the girls that it was alright to come over and they immediately circled him, barraging him with questions. Eleanor who had stopped some distance away was about to get off, too, when she saw a chubby little girl appear next to Blue's neck. She was about nine or ten years old, had a round face with freckles on the nose, equally round brown eyes and copper coloured short hair. She held out a hand for Blue to sniff.

"Hi Blueberry."

Then she smiled shyly at Eleanor.

"Hi. I'm Wendy."

"Hi. I'm Eleanor."

Wendy rolled her eyes.

"Yeah, I know."

"Hey Wendy," Pike called across, "would you show me where Casta's stable is, please?"

The little girl's eyes lit up when she heard him call her name and with her chest pushed out proudly she walked over to him. Before they could go anywhere, though, a male voice boomed across the yard from the entrance to the stable block.

"That won't be necessary. I'll take her in myself."

The girls lowered their heads and quickly made their way back to the manege. Wendy's shoulders slumped as she followed suit.

It was hard to see against the evening sun but Eleanor could make out the silhouette of a man approaching: tall and well built with the sleek movements of a body honed through a cross section of sports. As he came closer she could see that he was probably in his late forties or early fifties, a greying blonde with a full head of hair and a clear cut, well proportioned, if somewhat bland, face. His smile, as he crossed the yard, approaching boy and horse, was jovial.

"Peter. Good to see you. I'm glad you brought us Casta back. Sarah's already rung to tell me what's happened. What an awful bit of luck."

His speech doesn't sound right. It's not natural. It's stilted. Like he's had elocution lessons or something, Eleanor thought as she dismounted and led Blue closer to Pike and the Spanish mare.

The man was still a couple of meters away, when a pink metallic BMW convertible with the top down sped up the drive before coming to an abrupt halt, making Casta jump a little, although more out of habit than real fright it seemed. Whether it was being in familiar surroundings or whether it had been whatever had passed between the mare and her rider during the ride or simply the fact that she was tired after a long day, she appeared a different, much calmer horse now.

The female driver of the car, an older version of Tinkerbelle but with the colour of Wendy's hair and an unnaturally enhanced cleavage, put the handbrake on with a forcefulness that expressed undisguised anger. Eleanor had moved closer to Pike and Casta and caught him sneering at the man sarcastically.

"Look, Rob, your blow job's arrived. Better hop to it, eh?" A shadow moved across Robert Greaves' face and there was a sharp intake of breath but he was given no chance to retort as the surprisingly deep and sexy voice of Tinkerbelle's and Wendy's mother went into a loud rant, punctuated by her getting out of the car and slamming the door shut.

"What is *he* doing here?" she pointed at Pike, "And why is *she,*" the finger moved to Tinkerbelle in the arena, "still on a horse? – We've got to be at the Leylands' at seven.

And you all still need a shower. Now get her off that horse, Robert, and get in the fucking car, the lot of you!"
"Jennifer…" Robert Greaves started but she cut him short.
"Don't you Jennifer me. – Shift it, girls!" she shouted towards the arena.

Upon hearing her mother arrive Tinkerbelle had already halted and dismounted her horse and was now handing her instructor the reins. Without so much as a glance back, she moved out of the arena and in passing pointed at one of the spectating girls. The chosen one clapped her hands with joy and proceeded to the middle of the school, where she mounted the horse and began walking it around on a long rein.

Walking briskly towards her mum, Tinkerbelle took her hat and gloves off and handed them to her little sister at foot, who carried them without question yet all the while pulling a face, looking for Eleanor's eyes.

Eleanor gladly made contact.

Around the cluster of Robert Greaves, Jennifer Jones, Pike, Eleanor, Casta and Blue an awkward, cold silence had developed and when Tinkerbelle and Wendy arrived at the scene the temperature seemed to drop even further as Tinkerbelle looked Eleanor up and down before turning to Pike.

"Nice hat."

He smiled, unclipping the chin strap and taking it off.

"At least I carry it myself, eh."

Tinkerbelle turned to her mother.

"I'm ready."

The three Joneses started walking towards the car, leaving Robert Greaves suspended in action, torn between following them and taking Casta off Pike's hands as previously asserted. His decision was made for him as Jennifer reached the car and hissed at him loudly over her shoulder.

"Robert? – Now!"

He nodded to her sharply then turned to Pike.

"Stable fifteen. Let one of the girls show you where her tack goes."

Seconds later the BMW turned in the yard and sped down the drive, nearly knocking over a large girl in overalls with short, bleach blonde hair walking up from the road. Eleanor thought she could recognise the driver of the horsebox and the broad, warm smile stretching over Pike's face now told her she was right.

"Paytah," she shouted with enormous volume and stretched out arms.

"Here, grab these," Pike said shoving Casta's reins into Eleanor's hand and making towards the girl. Eleanor was left standing in between pony and horse, both of which had started dozing off, waiting patiently for the humans to sort them out.

"Char!" Pike called back to the girl, not quite as loudly but with equally open arms. When they met she put her massive arms around his hips and lifted him into the air. "You're back on a horse, man. Good boy!"

She set him down gently and punched him on the arm. Together they walked back to Eleanor. Next to him it became very clear that the girl must have been descended from giants.

From miniature giants but giants without a doubt, Eleanor thought.

She wasn't that terribly tall, although taller than Pike by a good few inches, but everything about her seemed super sized, not by an extra layer of fat but in solid muscle. Every detail about her seemed somewhat bigger than standard. At the same time her features were far from ugly, refined even - in a scaled up way. Within her largess she was immensely sensuous looking, with an enviable figure, beautifully curved lips and wide set, sparkling green eyes. When they arrived in front of Eleanor, Blue momentarily woke from her daze to greet her with a low nicker.

"Hey Blue," the girl greeted the pony back and let her nuzzle her palm.

She looked down at Eleanor.

"You're seriously miniscule."

Eleanor looked up.

"You're seriously ginormous."

The big girl laughed and punched Pike on the arm again. "Funny, that one. – Right," her gravelly voice suddenly sounded businesslike, "I'm supposed to be at the other side of the county in an hour, pick up some girlie from some show. Now that's not gonna happen, she's just gonna have to wait around, twiddling her rosettes. But – I can't be seen to take the piss either. So let's get her," she pointed at Casta, "put away and her," she pointed at Blue, "watered and shoved in the box and I drive you home on the way."

Pike looked at her aghast, shaking his head.

"I'm…"

"Save it," the girl said putting her hands up, "I get it, you're still not ready. You wanna walk, walk. Not a problem. But she," she said resolutely, stabbing the air with a finger in direction Blue again, "is going home in the box. - Look at her."

Eleanor knew without turning to face the pony what the big girl meant. Everything about the little mare exuded tiredness. Just standing next to her one could feel sheer exhaustion seeping off her. She sought Pike's eyes and knew he could see it, too.

While she waited with Blue for Pike and the big girl to return from putting Casta in her stable, the little mare drank in long gulps from a water bucket they had made one of the other girls fetch for her. Eleanor took the saddle off and put it on the ground, then rubbed the pony's sweaty back. Her thirst quenched, Blue raised her head just a few inches above the bucket and let the rest of the water dribble from her mouth. She breathed out a long sigh.

"It's alright, girl," Eleanor mumbled running her fingers along the muscles left and right of the pony's spine, "we're getting a lift home."

The big girl appeared on the other side.

"That's right," she said, "It's all first class from here. – I'm Charly by the way."

"Eleanor."

"You don't say."

"Where is Pike?"

"Clinging to the Spanish lady's neck, no doubt, drowning his sorrows. – He's coming," Charly answered, picking up the saddle, "Let's walk. He'll catch up. Let's hope the box is still there. I dumped it by the road - with the key still in the ignition."

Grinning, she led the way.

By the time Charly had loaded Blue, who'd eagerly walked up the ramp, letting out a long satisfied snort as she did so, Pike had indeed caught up.

He was in a funny mood, elated yet sad - on some level way less intense than Eleanor had ever experienced him before but at the same time totally raw.

They were standing by the side of the horsebox, silently watching Charly push up the ramp and click the locks into place. Suddenly Eleanor could feel his hand on her shoulder, his thumb brushing lightly against the side of her throat. She turned to face him.

"You go with them," he said quietly.

"Come with us?" Eleanor probed gently.

A faint smile gathered around his eyes.

"No," he said, "I'm...I need to walk."

Eleanor took a breath but he put a finger on her lips before she could say anything.

"Alone," he stated, took the finger away, kissed her and walked off.

Chapter 31

"He must really like you. I've never seen him like this. Maybe with Inara. But she was a horse," Charly cocked her head examining Eleanor's profile from across the cluttered middle seat of the horsebox's cab, "I know it's a cliché but you hurt him, I'll rip your heart out. And I mean that literally, you understand?"

There was a real threat here and Eleanor couldn't help but smirk, watching him in the distance, walking up a hill. She turned to meet the giantess' eyes.

"What are you smiling about?" Charly asked, taken aback.

"I'm just glad he has a friend."

Charly grunted and put the horsebox in gear.

"Not friend, sister," she said gruffly as they pulled away.

"What?"

Charly laughed.

"Ever hear Aaron talk about any snotty faced street urchins that Kimi and Karen used to take in? That'll be me. All of 'em. According to the old git I've eaten the rest. - I used to be fostered by them."

"Oh."

"He hasn't told you much, has he?"

Eleanor sighed.

"Pretty much nothing. - I wish he would."

"So what do you two talk about then?"

"Horses, mainly. Music. Books," Eleanor answered after a pause, then added quietly, "The merits of not killing yourself."

It took a long while for Charly to react. By the time she did they had entered the main road.

"I didn't realise it had got that bad," she said thoughtfully, her eyes firmly on the dense traffic ahead, "I knew suicidal tendencies were a symptom but I never thought of Paytah getting like that...." her voice trailed off.

"You called him that earlier."

"Called him what?"

"That thing you call him."

"Paytah? Cause that's his name, honey. His actual real name. In his passport like. Paytah Hawthorne. He hasn't told you that either, has he?" There was a certain glee in the big girl's voice that Eleanor didn't quite understand. "He changed it to Peter Pike when he moved to secondary. The Pike to piss off chickenshit John and the Peter because he had already got the shit ripped out of him left, right and centre at primary for being a boy that rides ponies, so he figured he didn't really need a Sioux name to add fuel to the fire, pardon the pun. That's what it means, fire. Peter Pike has a better ring to it though, sounds good in the show ring. But to me he will always be Paytah. And occasionally I still call him that. Just to wind him up. And it suits him. Kimi would be heartbroken to know he changed it. Her mum gave him that name, died the week after he was born. So not even chickenshit John could opt out of that one. That was before my time though. - I think it's stupid, this name changing business. You are who you are."

She switched on the radio with a resolute gesture, signalling the end of the conversation. Eleanor nestled back into the corner of the seat, leaning her head against the window and watching the evening sun bathe the hills in gold. She wondered how far he'd got on his journey back and whether he was alright. His kiss still burned on her lips. Thinking about it, her heart started racing again and the swarm of butterflies that inhabited her stomach these days fluttered up wildly.

They were crawling along to the subdued tune of some awful boy band or other and occasionally Eleanor could hear a clunk from the box behind them that made her flinch.

"Is she alright?" she finally asked.

Charly laughed a raspy laugh, grabbed a packet of tobacco from amongst the paraphernalia occupying the space between them and held it out to Eleanor.

"She's fine. She's done more trailer journeys than you and I have had hot dinners. I don't suppose you could do me a rollie, could you?"

Eleanor took the packet and smiled.

"I'll give it a go."

It took her full concentration but at the end of it she'd produced a passable roll up. After Charly took the first drag she breathed out contentedly.

"Not bad. You smoke?"

"No."

"Good. Best keep it that way. It's bloody expensive."

"Doesn't Greaves mind you smoking in here?"

"I'm sure he does. But I don't give a shit. The man's an arsehole of the highest order and I'm leaving anyway." Nevertheless, she rolled the window down a couple of inches and blew the smoke out through the gap.

"I don't get it," Eleanor burst out after a moment, "Pike hates the guy, you think he's an arsehole, why do you work for him?"

"It's a job. With horses. There aren't that many around here. It's all I know. Get to keep an eye on Strawberry that way, too. But more to the point when he and Karen split up he still owned half my ride. And he's been decent enough to let me work these past two years to buy him out. Only because she had a tendon injury, mind. So he thinks her competition days are over anyway," she blew out more smoke, "We'll show him."

Eleanor's jaw had dropped.

"They used to be *family*?"

Charly grinned knowingly, satisfied that the bombshell had indeed turned out to be just that.

"Well, no not directly. They weren't married or anything. They weren't even together that long. Though Robert was after Karen for years before she finally caved in. But in hindsight we reckon he wasn't after her at all, he was probably always after the land. You see, he doesn't really do horses, our Mr Greaves. Don't get me wrong, he's very athletic and a good enough rider but he's not a horse person. And the Black Horse is not how he makes his money. He owns a few care homes. Exclusive ones, like, you know, *nice* ones. Big business. The whole equestrian side is a tax write off if you ask me, though I don't understand enough about taxes and business to say that for sure. But I know that the Black Horse was a regular shit heap when he took it on. Now look at it. I mean, I've seen a fair few yards, you know. I can't think of another one, I mean a *working* one with lessons and shite, where the flower beds get weeded once a week. By a *gardner*. Actually coming to think of it, I can't think of a second one with flower beds."

She shrugged, taking another drag on her cigarette.

Suddenly Eleanor clicked.

"So he's the man who lent them all the money?"

Charly snorted.

"Not just a pretty face, are ya?"

Something in all of this bothered Eleanor but she couldn't quite put her finger on it. Then it dawned on her.

"Maybe he just likes taking stuff that's falling apart and putting it right?" Eleanor offered.

"Oh my god, the little bro has found himself an optimist," Charly burst out in genuine laughter, "Sorry but if you knew Robert Greaves you'd laugh, too. No, honey, Rob does nothing because he 'just likes'. There always has to be money, or even better, status, in there somewhere. Otherwise he would have given Karen some reprieve. But he hasn't. His stance is, he's taking the land and that's that."

"Shit," Eleanor let slip.

The way the events of the day had unfolded had felt so much like a beginning rather than an end that it had unwittingly fanned her hopes of there being some last ditch solution. The idea that it could all finish so abruptly, on such a high note, just felt plain wrong.

"Shit indeed," Charly echoed.

They sat in silence for a while.

Eleanor could hardly bring herself to ask but in the end she had to.

"So do you reckon he's going to put a care home on it?"

Charly shook her head violently.

"No chance. That road's the most expensive in the whole town. Most of the people who live on it are involved in running the fucking place in some way or another. They wouldn't have it. No, not a care home. I'm fairly sure he wants to put a nice fat house on it - for him, his bitch and her puppies. Sorry, that's unfair, Wendy is actually a really nice kid. Word goes, he's been trying to buy up a property in that road forever and a day. That's how he first came to the cottage, years ago, with an offer to buy them out. Hadn't counted on chickenshit John's hard nut though. You see, in his head he hasn't made it until he has a house on *that* road. He is completely self made, Rob, you gotta give him that. Comes from scum, proper bottom of the barrel - and I can say that, I come from the layer just below, you know, the gunk at the bottom of the bottom. If it wasn't for the Pikes and the Hawthornes I wouldn't be able to read, let alone have a Diploma. I'd be dead or in prison by now, talking about keeping up family traditions…" her voice trailed off and she sighed deeply.

Eleanor had started recognising their surroundings now. They were approaching Hawthorne Cottage from the other side, passing through the woodland on the main road from nowhere. The track had changed on the radio a few times and suddenly Eleanor recognised the first couple of chords of *Sea of Life.* Charly's hand darted forward to turn up the volume.

"Brilliant," she exclaimed, "I love this song. Have you heard this? Normally I don't like all this folk shite, I'm more into Punk and Ska, but this is awh...I downloaded the album and you know, she might actually turn me into an acoustic guitar loving, tree hugging idiot. And she is gorgeous. Possibly the most beautiful woman alive. What a babe."

Eleanor smiled and looked out of the window, singing along quietly to the song. She spoke up just before the last chords faded away, her eyes still on the world outside. "Did you know she is playing The Depot tomorrow night?"

They had arrived and Charly put the indicator on to signal she was pulling up to the curb by the twitten.

"Yes I know," she answered dismayed as she stopped the engine, "but I only discovered her about five days ago. Tickets have been sold out for weeks."

Eleanor carried on staring at the dark gap between the flint stone wall encompassing Hawthorne Cottage and the corner of the hedgerow. Suddenly it *did* feel like an ending, coming back here, where the journey had begun, knowing it would soon look different.

She thought of all the people involved in this summer and where they were right now. Of Pike walking over the hills on his own having finally ridden a horse again; of Kjell, Isabel and the brand new entity Oscar probably sitting at home in the garden, enjoying the last of the evening sun contented in their little unit; of Aaron and Sarah, in all likelihood still in a waiting room at the hospital; of Ebony, probably getting ready in some backstage area somewhere in another town not too far from this one - and for once she also thought of herself.

I'm going to be alright, whatever happens.

She turned to Charly who was patiently waiting for her to spring into action.

"You could come with us, you know. To the gig."

"What?" Charly looked at her astonished, "You got a spare ticket?"

"Better," Eleanor grinned, "We're on the guest list – Pike, mum and me. And we can always bring a plus one. - Ebony is a friend."

"You're kidding me!"

"Nope," Eleanor couldn't resist it, "He hasn't told you much, has he?"

Chapter 32

Eleanor was sitting on the upturned crate in the stable block aisle, still waiting for his return, when her phone rang. She took a sip from the water bottle she'd been rolling between her hands before she dug into her pocket to fish it out.

Half past seven already, she thought as she put it to her ear, *where is he? Surely he should be back by now.*

"Hi mum," she said into the receiver without having bothered to check the display. This was their daily routine now.

"Hi hon, how are you doing? Coming home tonight?" Eleanor didn't know what to say. She was exhausted and she'd just been over to the cottage again where nobody was in still. Part of her just wanted to go home, have a shower, have some food, snuggle into bed - and sleep. Another part desperately wanted to be here when he came back. She looked around the empty barn and through the open doors out onto the paddock, where Blue was lazing in the red glow of the evening sun. She felt lost here on her own so late in the day. She also knew if her mum knew she was out in the barn alone at this time, she'd have kittens. She sighed.

"No," she finally answered.

Isabel echoed her sigh.

"I know it's a radical idea but occasionally I would quite like to see my daughter?" There was a distracted air to it, as if she was simultaneously typing on the computer or looking at post.

"I know, mum. But I...tonight I want to be here."

"Hm," Isabel had temporarily put aside whatever was cutting her attention in half and was focusing on the conversation now, "you know, Peter could always stay here, too. I don't mind. Makes no difference whether you are sharing a bed here or there. It's not that big a deal if you two take it slowly. Although I would prefer it if you waited for the whole shebang till it was at least legal. But the way it looks to me," her attention suddenly waned again and this time Eleanor could actually hear papers being shuffled, "we're all in this for the long haul, so it might be nice to occasionally have him here. - Although come next Thursday and school starts again, you two are going to have to restrict your sleepovers to weekends."

Eleanor smiled. She knew it *was* a big deal for her mum and she was grateful. Up to now they had not actually spoken about the fact that Eleanor had never as much as spent one night in a guest room at Hawthorne Cottage. And although everyone seemed to know their business better than Eleanor and Pike themselves, which was mildly to moderately embarrassing, it did feel good to have it out in the open.

"So you trust me now then, do you?"

"Not remotely," Isabel answered with a grin in her throat, "but," she sighed, "rather under my or Aaron's roof than on the back seat of some shitty car."

"First I'd have to get him into a shitty car," Eleanor stated matter-of-factly.

"Pardon? I missed that." Oscar had started crying in the background.

"Never mind. Not important. Tomorrow, yeah? After the gig. I'll ask him to stay over at ours. And mum?"

"Yes, hon?"

"I love you."

"I love you, too, baby."

It was nearly nine o'clock, the sun had set and even the twilight was fading to dark now, when, to her great relief, Eleanor finally saw light at the cottage as she approached. She had spent the last hour wandering back and forth between barn and house, trying to ring first Pike, whose phone had been switched off as pretty much always, and then Aaron who hadn't answered either and she had started to wonder whether maybe she needed to ring home, own up and get herself collected.

Aaron seemed more than surprised to see her when he answered the door with uncharacteristic cheerfulness.

"Eleanor," he looked around over her shoulder, "where is Peter?"

Eleanor shrugged.

"I don't know. He walked home. Blue and I got a lift."

"Yes. With Charlene, I know. He rang to tell me all was well."

A frown formed on the old man's forehead.

"Is he not back yet?"

Eleanor shook her head. Hearing Aaron ask the question, suddenly made her worry properly.

Where are you?

"And you've been here on your own all this time?"

Eleanor nodded. Aaron shook his head in disapproval.

"I'm not keen on that," he suddenly seemed to realise that they were still standing on the doorstep, "Well, come on in, little lady – I'm just heating some soup for Sarah and me, come join us," as Eleanor moved past him, he gently squeezed her shoulder, "Don't you worry, he'll be back soon enough."

An enticing smell emanated from the pot on the Aga and Eleanor instantly became aware of a growling hunger in her stomach. Sarah was sitting at the kitchen table, the top of which was covered in old photo albums and scrap books. Her arm was encased in a temporary cast and resting in a foam sling. She looked totally at home here and Eleanor who had noticed two suitcases at the bottom of the stairs as she'd come through, realised swiftly that the older woman was here to stay.

"Eleanor, my saviour. Come sit with me," Sarah said and shuffled up the bench to make space. Eleanor sidled up to her.

"You staying?"

Sarah nodded with an embarrassed smile. "Indefinitely. - Aaron insisted."

"Couldn't have one of the crew stay in that flea-ridden cesspit of a bedsit. No way, not on my watch," Aaron said gruffly with his back to them, while stirring the soup, "I don't understand why you did not get in touch when you came back to the country, to be honest. You must have known Kimi's and my doors would always be open to you. And it's not like we are hard to find."

"It's been thirty odd years, Aaron."

"Thirty years, thirty minutes," he turned to face them, blowing on the spoon before tasting the soup, "what difference does it make? Friends are friends, crew is crew. – It's nearly ready. Eleanor could you push those up the other end, please?" he said, indicating the albums.

As Eleanor was about to shut the open scrapbook in front of her, her eyes fell on a yellowed newspaper clipping.

'Wild West goes to town' the rather naff headline read, below which was a picture of two smiling young women with arms over each others shoulder: one a beautiful blonde in a showgirl's headdress, the other a dark haired, dark skinned, dark eyed, broad faced woman, dressed as a squaw. Eleanor did a double take.

"Oh my word, that's you!" she exclaimed, pointing at the blonde.

"Uhu," Sarah answered, "and that's Kimi," she pointed at the squaw girl, "that was one of our first acts together. After we met on the set of some spaghetti western she convinced me to come and join the show."

Eleanor took a moment to study the dead woman's face. *She looks the real deal.*

She also looked remarkably like her grandson and Eleanor couldn't help but feel anxious again. Just then a bowl of soup appeared in her vision. She shut the scrapbook quickly, putting it with the others at the end of the table. For the next ten minutes Eleanor was all mouth and belly. Nothing else mattered – until they heard the front door open and close, followed by footsteps going up the stairs. Eleanor could feel the heavy door to the watchtower being opened above their heads and when it fell shut, looked from Aaron to Sarah and back. They'd all stopped in their tracks as an unmistakable cloud of sadness and despair had crept along the floorboards and reached their ankles. Aaron who'd only just served himself and sat down, made to get up again but Eleanor gently shook her head. She looked down at her half finished soup, took a deep breath and got up.

The room was stuffy from the day's accumulated heat. He'd stripped down to his boxer shorts and was lying on the bed in a foetal position with his face turned towards the wall, clinging to his duvet and sobbing uncontrollably. He hadn't acknowledged Eleanor, who had silently entered the room, in any way. She was standing next to the bed, looking down at him. As she hesitantly put a hand on his shoulder the sobs became more violent and he crawled deeper into himself but didn't shake her off. Finding it difficult to breathe in here, she took her hand away to navigate the clutter on the floor across to the window. She opened it and felt the cool evening air spread over her face and past her into the room. She turned to walk back, bringing the breeze with her. Looking down at him again, she could feel her heart beat speeding up, knowing what she was about to do. Pushing all thought aside, she took her clothes off until she, too, was naked down to her pants and slipped in behind him. She slung one arm around his waist and slithered the other under the side of his neck, pushing her naked torso up against the smooth skin of his back. He was hot to the touch and she knew she was wrapping him like a cold flannel, holding him as wave after wave of tears kept rippling through his body.

Up to this moment she'd always considered him so much older than her, so much more capable, so much more sure of who and what he was and where he stood in the world. As he lay in her arms now, weeping for his dead horse and the life he'd lost, he felt like just a boy. Just as bewildered and struggling as her, as every other kid on the planet, whatever their story.

She lightly blew some air against the nape of his neck where her mouth was resting and smiled in the knowledge that amongst all the pain, the one shiver going through him just then was one of joy and not sorrow.

After that she let him be, holding him tight, a hand on his heart until he'd cried himself to sleep and she followed suit, letting unconsciousness engulf her.

Chapter 33

"We were coming back from a show."

His voice cut clearly through the stillness of the night and Eleanor felt herself being catapulted back into the room, as if awakened from a hypnotic state by a click of the fingers. It was still dark outside and she had no idea how much time had passed since they'd fallen asleep. They had remained in the same position, though at one point he had obviously released the duvet from the grip of his legs and thrown it over both of them before cupping her hand resting on his chest in his own.

"I had a really bad feeling about it before we even left here. It was a really shitty day. You know, when you have one of those when absolutely everything just goes wrong? You know, you step on the rake then kick over the water bucket and your pony spooks and jumps on your foot. That kind of day," he sighed deeply then carried on, "It was the first show we were signed up to do after Inara had had her foal. He was only four months old, poor sod, but some people wean them that early and it was just a local thing, not even a whole day, just a small midweek event. For charity. We were supposed to be in and out in a couple of hours. 'Show our faces, get a couple of rosettes, go home' Karen said," he sniffled and held Eleanor's hand more tightly, "So we went. With the old trailer. Just Inara and us. The others were coming directly from the Black Horse that day. – You got to know, they were seeing each other then, Karen and Robert. And Blue lived over there for the summer, with Straw, nannying some yearling. She was already half retired but Wendy was riding her then," Eleanor could feel a stab of jealousy and he squeezed her hand lightly, somehow knowing what she felt, "Blue was taking her off the lead rein. They were supposed to do a first ridden class that day. I think they actually did. I don't even know. She is good at that, Blue. Looks after children.

And Wendy is a nice kid. She's got it. The thing Tink hasn't - empathy, the link. Tinkerbelle looks good on a horse, knows the aids, Wendy is a rider. We were practically family, you know. All of us. Karen and Jenny have been friends…forever. *Were* friends. They went to school together. When Jenny split up with Tink's dad they even lived here with us for a while. Tink was still really tiny and they had nowhere else to go. Till Jenny found Wendy's dad to take care of them. My nan was still alive then. I don't really remember it much but I remember her always being wary of Jenny, saying she was just looking for a meal ticket. - She was good at reading people, my nan. People and horses," he paused, "I really miss her." Eleanor suddenly felt crowded, as if all these people, all this past he had been holding off so forcefully was now crashing in on them with a vengeance. She could feel an impulse inside of her making her want to shout: *'Stop! Make them go away again. Let's stay huddled in the present, just you and me.'*

But she knew that while ignorance might have been bliss it was not an option any longer.

So instead she pushed up against him, even closer than before, burying her face in between his shoulder blades, feeling her breath ricochet off his skin and bracing herself for the rest. It was a long while before he finally continued, still addressing the wall.

"We all assumed they'd get married, Karen and Rob. And – he wasn't bad for her. Grandpa didn't like him much but Rob made her happy, at least for a while," he sighed, "So we get to the show and we park up and Karen goes to find them. And she does. She finds Rob in the cab of a truck, with Jenny…" his voice trailed off uncomfortably.

"Giving him a blow job," Eleanor finished the sentence in a whisper.

She could feel him nod. Tears were choking his voice again when he carried on.

"So we left again. I mean, I never even got to unload Inara. Karen was back within minutes. Furious, angry, crying, swearing - I'd never seen her like that. If you knew Karen…she's like the most level-headed person on the planet. Nothing fazes her. I should have stopped her, shouldn't have let her drive in that state. But I said nothing. Just got in the passenger seat and off we went, back home." He took a deep breath, let go of her hand, exhaled slowly and then turned to face her, seeking her hand again immediately. Their fingers interlaced as they looked at each other in the dark.

"You know the bridge just up from the estuary, the other side of town?" he asked, calmly now.

Eleanor shook her head.

"Anyway, that's where it happened. - Karen was still bawling her eyes out and she was driving too fast. Swerved. Not much, really, but she wasn't thinking straight, reacted all wrong. Next thing I know, we've crashed and I've got a face full of glass. I look behind me and the trailer's gone," he shut his eyes, "Just gone. The tow ball failed. The whole thing just came off, crashed though the barrier and down into the water," silent tears were running down his cheeks now, "So I crawled out, through the glass and I could hear Inara. She was still *alive* then. The trailer hadn't sunk yet and she was thrashing and whinnying. In that metal box. - I tried to get to her," he was sobbing again, "but by the time I got down there, it was too late. I went in anyway, nearly drowned. *Did* drown," he swallowed, opened his eyes again, "they had to resuscitate me. - And every single day afterwards I wished they hadn't. They put me on medication. They put me in therapy. They even put me in a self help group for young adults with PTSD. Full of soldiers. Nineteen year old guys, just back from a war zone. And me. The silly little boy with the dead horse. That's when I made up my

189

mind," he disentangled his fingers from hers and began caressing her face, "Then you come along."

She shuffled up to him, close enough for their noses to touch.

Something fundamental had shifted.

She allowed herself to long for him now, could feel herself burning brighter inside with every stroke of his fingertips.

Kiss me, she willed him. *Please.*

He laughed that quiet, knowing laugh of his.

"One day," he said, "you might want to try saying what you want out loud, Eleanor."

One day, she thought but didn't get further as he yielded to her request with a lot more passion than she had anticipated.

When she woke late the next morning she found herself alone in the bed, feeling happily woozy, her mouth and tongue still numb from all the kissing, her core still squishy with lust. They hadn't been able to take their mouths and hands off each other until dawn had already turned into day, when they had finally succumbed to slumber, still holding each other tight. There had been more than one point when she could easily have given in to her body's instincts if he had pushed it but instead he had retracted every time she had started straining against him, shushing her, his hands becoming instantly soothing rather than rousing.

Now, in the stark light of day, she was grateful for his restraint, knowing instinctively that she would have regretted rushing things, despite being sure of the person.

"We have time," was the last thing he'd whispered in her ear, before they'd surrendered to sleep.

She smiled at the memory and blessed her luck.

Somewhere, in the twilight zone between life and death, she'd found herself the one in a million.

She got up and walked over to the open window looking out onto the sunny day. The air already smelled lightly of autumn now and soon the leaves would turn. She scanned the paddock for the shape of the pony she was going to have to say goodbye to soon and found her grey outline, lying flat on her side in her favourite ditch. The energy around her still seemed low, exhausted from the strains of the previous day, and for a moment Eleanor's heart stopped, convinced the little mare had lain down to die. Then, suddenly, the pony's head rose up, quick as lightening, to bite some flies away from her tummy before flopping back down again. Eleanor grinned. The little grand dame of Hawthorne Barn was far from finished. Nevertheless, Eleanor decided, the previous day's ride would have been their last.

'Always go out on a high,' she heard her grandmother's advice through the ether.

I should ring you, Eleanor thought, *tell you what's happened. Ask about the foot.*

Just then she heard laughter and voices rise from the back garden below. She couldn't see from here what was happening down there and went to investigate.

Chapter 34

Passing the kitchen on the way out, Eleanor caught a glimpse of emptiness in the corner of her eye and did a double take. The table had been removed and the chairs were gone, only the L-shaped bench remained somewhat forlorn in the corner.

The mystery was solved when she got to the open back door and looked out onto the garden, where Pike was sitting at the dragged-out kitchen furniture amidst the remnants of a buffet type breakfast, leafing through the albums that had apparently been moved out here along with the table, chairs and Aaron.

Sarah was crouching on the ground by the wall, liberating what appeared to be an old vegetable patch by pulling up bindweed with her good hand and flinging it over her shoulder in a heap. All the while she was gently berating Aaron who was standing next to her with amused eyes, leaning heavily on his walking stick and sipping a cup of tea.

"Honestly, Aaron, how can an outside plant like you keep on hiding in a scullery and let this go to pot. You really want to get out here from time to time and look after your patch."

Pike looked up at Eleanor and smiled, his eyes reflecting the yellow of the midmorning sun as a mellow flickering amber. He pulled out the chair next to him and gathered up the spread out food stuffs, putting them in a circle around the untouched plate that had been laid out for her. "Hungry?" he asked when she arrived next to him.

"Ravenous," she answered as she sat down and grabbed a roll, looking around the offerings, "Very continental."

"All her," Pike pointed at Sarah then added in a sniggering whisper, "She made him get on the bus with her and go to the supermarket this morning. And guess what."

"What?" Eleanor whispered back with a sly glance, playing along to the conspiracy.

"He even forgot to take his stick," he whispered in her ear, then brushed his lips against the soft part just behind her ear lobe. She shivered, instantly wishing the two of them back into the night. She held her breath for a moment to even out her heart beat again.

"Pike…" she said turning to face him but her voice trailed off. She'd been about to say *thank you,* when suddenly it felt all wrong. She frowned and looked into his eyes, studying the red sparks firing off in the sea of yellow, like perpetual fireworks.

"Yeah?" There was apprehension in his voice now because for once he couldn't read her mind. She could feel the fear of rejection coming off him so strongly, she wanted to hug him tight and squeeze it out like a bad boil. She found his hand under the table and he exhaled, visibly relieved.

"I can't call you that anymore," she stated, grinning mischievously before adding more quietly, so that Aaron and Sarah wouldn't hear, "I'm not posh enough to be snogging a surname."

He laughed.

"How about just calling me by my name then?"

"Paytah?"

He flinched.

"Nobody has really called me that in a very long time," he said in a subdued tone.

"True," Aaron's voice cut in. They had been so engrossed in their exchange, they hadn't notice him approach. Presently he was standing next to Eleanor, undressing the tea pot from its cosy, about to pour Eleanor a cup, "But it is bloody well time, somebody did. – If you keep denying who you are, the spell *will* fail."

He had said the last part with more emphasis than Eleanor had ever heard him speak before and she looked inquisitively from man to boy and back. Aaron shook his head and nodded towards his grandson, who raised his hands in a warding off gesture and got up. Half way, he put his hands on the table, leant forward and addressed Eleanor with the occasional sarcastic side glance at Aaron. "Call me what you will. But don't listen to him. All people go a bit funny in old age but horse people are the worst. Cut above even mad cat ladies. – I'm going to check on Blue. Grab yourself some breakfast, see me in the barn."

And off he went.

She found them in the ditch, Blue still lying on her side and him propped up against her spine, his long legs stretched out in front of him, his head tilted back to rest on the bulk of the pony's body, eyes shut against the glaring sunlight. They were breathing in unison. Eleanor slowed down as she approached, not wanting to disturb the picture, the perfect peace they seemed to be at, yet burning with curiosity still. She hadn't been able to get another word out of Aaron and in the end had grabbed a second roll and made off to follow him. She swallowed and shoved the last bite into her mouth.

"It's funny," he began loudly, without opening his eyes, talking up into the air, "most of the time I can hear you think even two miles up the road - and then other times I haven't got a clue what goes on in that brain of yours. Why is that?"

"What about now?" she asked, sitting down opposite him some distance away, legs crossed.

He lifted his head off the mare, which evoked an annoyed swish of the tail against the ground from the pony, and looked at Eleanor.

"Forget it, Eleanor. It's horseshit."

"You can still tell me though, can't you? – Paytah," she was playing with the sound of it and the way it rolled off her tongue.

"Man, you can be a real pain in the butt," he said, grinning widely, chipped incisor flashing at her, "Alright. So the story goes that my great-grandmother, no, hang on," he mumbled something, counting down fingers, "my great-great-grandmother put a spell on this land. As long as her descendents, oh, and the descendents of her horse - very important this bit, otherwise it wouldn't be horseshit, right? It would just be plain bollocks – anyway, as long as they proudly walk this land, it can't be taken away from them."

"And you don't believe in it?" Eleanor tried to sound as evenly as possible.

"Don't be absurd."

"Hm," she carried on undeterred before adding thoughtfully, "but Blue isn't one of those descendents, right?"

"No," he took a deep breath, "Not you as well, please. Do me a favour!"

"You believe in Pixies..." she grinned apologetically.

"Sprites," he corrected her softly, "and just in the one, actually."

She wondered for a moment how it could be possible that someone could make your heart skip a beat with just the drop of a voice and half a sentence.

"But you see," he continued, the tone all sarcasm now, "Sprites are a British invention, meaning they might even work. My great-great-grandmother was Oglala Sioux. Came here with Buffalo Bill in eighteen-ninety-something-or-other. You can look it up. Ran away. With her horse. Long story. It was lame, they were going to shoot it. She took it and scarpered. In the middle of the October storms. Hid out in the woods over there. That's where my great-great-grandfather found her, a month or so later. Almost frozen to death. Let grandpa tell you some time. He loves all that shit. Point being, true or not – if Sioux mumbo jumbo could really save your land, the last couple of hundred years of North American history would have looked somewhat different, don't you think?"

There was so much venom in the way he spoke, the pony's tail had started pounding the earth and she was now making to get up. He shuffled away from her, stretching out a pacifying hand but the little mare shook it off. Once up she looked at him angrily, ears back, neck hanging low, snorted at him in disapproval and wandered off. He pulled a face after her, before turning back to Eleanor and carrying on, more subdued now but still angry.

"Have you ever tried typing Sioux into the computer? Of course not, why would you. - Basically, the net starts vomiting despair at you. Site after site on stolen land, poverty, murder, alcoholism, teenage suicide and hopelessness."

You ever tried searching 'midget'?

She didn't say it out loud though. Somewhere amidst his rant she'd started, not for the first time in recent weeks, hearing her mum's voice in the back of her head. *'It's all about their chaos and their joy and their pain and their soul searches and their creativity and their self esteem or lack thereof.'* But just then, as she began to wonder once more, his face broke into an apologetic smile.

"Sorry, it really bugs me, this spell crap," he said softly, "What about you? What do you want to do with the last of days? Last ride?"

The way he put it made her suddenly acutely aware again of the lump of ice that had lodged itself in her stomach all those weeks ago, when he had first told her that it would come to this, and that had never truly dissolved. Hiding below joy, passion and other fears, it had always been there - a cold chunk of preserved pain, waiting in the freezer compartment of her soul, about to be defrosted.

"No," she responded resolutely, cleaning some dirt from under her fingernails. Then she looked up to smile back at him. "Yesterday was good. Let's leave it."

Her eyes wandered over to the grazing pony who was still clearly annoyed, swishing her tail violently, almost stomping her feet as she moved from grass patch to grass patch, crinkling up her nose in search of the choicest blades. Eleanor could feel tears form in the back of her throat but forced them back down. There would be plenty of time for crying the next day. And the next. And the next.

Suddenly she felt like she had to get out of here, to get some distance between herself and Hawthorne Barn, to find some strength in another reality to face the morrow. She took a deep breath and sought his eyes again.

"Besides, we've been doing your world all summer. Let's do mine today. You might find that without bossing me about on a pony all day, you might not even like me."

It had been supposed to be a joke but she could see a flicker of real pain pass in the flames.

"Or," he retorted coldly, "you might find that without a pony for you to ride, I'm only half as interesting."

She laughed it off.

"No chance," she crawled over to him and brought her face up to his, "do you realise, Paytah, that you've never even seen my room?"

His smile reached all the way up to his eyes this time.

"I thought you'd never ask."

Chapter 35

She'd only hoped for a bit of an escape but it would turn out to be one of the best days of her life.

The thought had never crossed her mind that he could have been as intrigued by her as she had been by him but as they sat in her room, going through her boxes of mementos while she told him where in the world she had been and who she had met, she soon realised that his eyes were not just growing bigger and bigger as she carried on but that he was also immensely grateful to be let in.

It was a strange sensation.

She was so used to feeling ashamed of admitting to other kids how well travelled she was and how much she'd seen, fearing they would think her a liar or, worse, an arrogant little shit that the warmth with which he received her stories made her question how often in the past she'd missed out on true friendship by being cagey. She said as much and he grinned.

"No, they'd probably have thought you were a liar - or an arrogant little shit," he said teasingly before scooping her up into his arms to pull her backwards onto his lap. He cradled her from behind and whispered into her ear how envious he was.

Playing with her hands, he told her that he'd been all around the British Isles for shows but had never left the country. The horses had always come first. His dream had been to break convention; to break through the ranks of the squeaky clean riders on their shiny, big bay European Warmbloods; to work with Inara towards being the first person ever to end up at the Olympic Games with a coloured American Indian Horse. He had been going to astonish them all and gain recognition for the agile, intelligent if somewhat small breed that was so inextricably woven into the fibre of his very existence. He snorted an 'as if' there, shaking his head at his own deluded naivety, then shrugged it off. That was then, this was now.

Eleanor noticed how, with the mystery lifted, he seemed to be able to just talk about the past frankly and factually now, full of emotion but not with utter despair. For a moment she wondered whether maybe the loss of the land would come as a relief to him.

When she asked him, he didn't respond immediately, actually taking his time to think about it. Finally she could feel him shaking his head behind hers.

"Maybe it will, maybe it won't. But if we were to find a briefcase with the money in it today, I wouldn't exactly go and try to find the mafia boss it belongs to. I'd make sure it appears in Rob's account by midnight on Monday, make no mistake."

Just then they noticed Isabel and Oscar standing in the open door to the room and he raised Eleanor's right hand to wave at them, making her giggle. Isabel smiled wistfully, before asking them down for lunch.

After that, they let the whole subject lie completely, leaving for the beach and immersing themselves in the present. Eating ice cream, playing "spot-the" games, running barefoot in the sea, building pebble castles and occasionally stealing a kiss. Until it was time to head for The Depot.

The Depot lay under the promenade at the end of the arches, where it had once served as the storage space for the electric railway that ran along the coast in the summer. It was an odd choice of venue for a folk gig since it normally hosted rock and punk bands as the many withered posters plastered on the columns along the way would testify.

Charly was already waiting for them, clearly at home here, chatting to a couple of bouncers, while having a smoke. They'd come early and there weren't any other people about yet. Eleanor could feel the boy next to her getting quite nervous as they approached. It was his first gig – a concept she could hardly fathom.

She elbowed him gently.

"You're gonna be fine, it's *folk* for heaven's sake. And look, we've got our own bodyguard and all," she said nodding at the giantess.

Charly looked gorgeous. Out of her overalls, in civilian punk chic and with no make up bar a dark berry red lipstick to accentuate her fabulous lips she could have been straight out of some cool underground flick. She grinned widely from Eleanor to Pike and back when they reached her, then put a hefty hand on the small girl's shoulder.

"You, Miss, are one amazing chick. – Now lead the way." Eleanor looked up at the bouncers.

"We're on the guest list. Eleanor McGraw, Peter Pike and this," she pointed at Charly, "is our plus one."

The men looked down at her, obviously torn between being amused at what they thought was panache and being hacked off because she was clearly only the first of a long line of punters today who would attempt to take the piss. Before they could respond though, Eleanor sighed, putting up a hand.

"Save it. Just go check with the door guy."

They didn't just go and check, they brought the door guy with them. He was a bug eyed, grey bearded biker type in leather trousers, a lumberjack shirt and a chained up wallet, who was studying a clipboard as he came through the door.

"Yup," he said, looking up and unclipping three backstage passes, handing them out but withholding Eleanor's for a moment, his forehead furrowed, studying her face intently, "although, technically I can't really let *you* in until your mum's here."

Eleanor took a deep breath, about to protest when the man's face broke into a warm smile.

"You don't recognize me, do you? - I didn't expect you to. You were tiny when we last met. My name's Toby. I used to roadie for your dad? I – " he added grinning, pointing at himself and then jabbing lightly at her shoulders, "even changed your nappies once or twice. My claim to fame that is, changing Jerry McGraw's baby daughter's nappies," he laughed, "works with the ladies every time. Better than saying I've held Mick Jagger's dick, which isn't true by the way. – Here, enjoy."

Eleanor smiled awkwardly as he put the pass over her head. She couldn't remember ever feeling as embarrassed this side of growing out of wetting the bed.

It was a good while later - they were sitting backstage drinking tea, much to Charly's bemusement who had left them to stand behind the stage, mesmerised by Ebony sound checking - when the encounter came back to haunt her.

She had felt his eyes on her profile for a good minute or so, not turning to face him, knowing full well what was about to come out of his mouth. It had been the one piece of information she had withheld, purposefully, knowing his music collection contained pretty much the entire back catalogue of her father's records, including tracks she'd never even heard of before she'd set foot in the watchtower. She didn't know why it felt so awkward, why she would have liked to have kept these two parts of her reality separate.

"Jerry McGraw?" he raised his voice over the music, all played up disbelief.

"Uhu," she nodded, still not facing him.

"*The* Jerry McGraw?"

"Uhu," for some reason it made her smile. She took a sip of her tea.

"I know you said your father was the best guitar player in the world. I didn't realise you *meant* it."

"Hm."

"Wow." He leant back in his chair and suddenly she could hear him think very loudly, his foot twitching hectically. She also knew he would never, in a billion years, actually ask.

"Forget it," she answered the unmentioned, still staring at the opaque liquid in her mug, "I already had the conversation. He's broke. Famous doesn't mean business savvy as mum always says."

His foot instantly stopped tapping as he leant forward, took her chin and turned her towards him.

"Thank you, Eleanor McGraw."

"What for?"

"Trying."

He kissed her gently but before they could pick up where they had left off somewhere on the beach, there was a lull in the music and they heard someone nearby loudly clearing her throat. Isabel was standing behind them, eyebrows raised. Eleanor contemplated for a moment what it was that appeared strange about her mother until she realised she wasn't wearing Oscar but carrying her violin case instead.

"Hi mum," Eleanor grinned, "you look weird without a baby."

"Yes," her mum retorted, "and you would look weird *with* one. You remember that, you two."

Eleanor blushed.

"You playing?" she swiftly changed the subject.

"Not just playing," her mum's face transformed into a devilish grin, "I've been challenged to a proper duel no less. Now, where do I get a cuppa tea around here?"

The gig turned out to be a triumph, with Ebony effortlessly convincing each and every audience member, even those who'd come sceptical of a one hit wonder, of her talent and the fun that could be had in modern folk music.

Isabel, who had, of course, come up trumps in the fiddle duel and who, much to her feigned surprise, had been invited by Ebony to follow it up with *Kittens in the Den,* glowed with satisfaction on the way home in the cab. They had set out directly after the last encore, leaving the Scottish goddess in the capable hands of a totally smitten Charly, promising to show her the seaside nightlife and the best time ever.

Eleanor would have liked to have stayed a while to catch up but Isabel, despite being in high spirits, had been anxious to get back to her baby, which she claimed she could hear cry all the way from across town. Her commanding demeanour, fuelled by a primeval urge to get back to her young, had not even left room for Pike to argue his way out of stepping into the taxi.

So he'd held Eleanor's hand the entire way, squeezing it hard each time they turned a corner.

When they arrived at the house, they heard as soon as they shut the cab doors that Isabel had been perfectly right about her baby's demands. Most of the street was being left in no doubt as to how powerful Oscar's little lungs were.

A dishevelled Kjell cradling a beetroot red, exceptionally angry baby boy opened the front door to them. Without further ado, Isabel swapped violin case for child and scurried off to settle down on the nearest settee to feed him. Kjell, Eleanor and Pike were still standing on the door step when the screams subsided. Kjell let out a long breath.

"He just wouldn't have it," he told them with vacant, exhausted eyes, "kept spitting out the bottle. Wants it au naturel only. – Sorry," he added, stepping aside to unblock the doorway, "come on in. There is some lasagne in the oven, if you're hungry."

After food they sat with Isabel, a now happily sleeping Oscar and Kjell in the living room, chatting about the gig and how well Ebony had looked before Eleanor and Pike finally made their excuses.

The weirdest thing is, Eleanor thought to herself as she was kissing her mum goodnight to go upstairs with him, *that it doesn't even feel weird.*

Chapter 36

Moving through crisp autumn air, they were once again walking the entire way hand in hand, alas in the other direction. Though finding solace in each other's company they were both too raw to talk, too sad to do anything but put one foot in front of the other. This time around nobody was marching anyone and no one felt protected from harm.

It was early morning.

His phone, switched on for once, had declared the reception of a text around 1am, announcing the safe arrival of Karen at Hawthorne Cottage with the request to see her nephew for breakfast.

Isabel and Kjell had offered to drive them but they had kindly declined without having to discuss it between them, each knowing as well as the other that they needed to approach this at their own pace – to slowly run at it on their own feet, not be transported to it.

They weren't far now and Eleanor could feel the familiar pressure on the sides of her hand as he squeezed it gently.

"Thank you for coming with me, Eleanor," he said quietly without stopping.

Eleanor looked at their shoes against the pavement, covering ground.

"She is my pony." It had slipped out without her thinking about it and she heard him draw a sharp breath. A hand flew up to her mouth and she looked at him sideways.

"I'm sorry," she spluttered apologetically, "I didn't..I...I-"

He squeezed her hand again reassuringly and carried on walking.

"It's alright," he cut in, eyes searching the road ahead, "The thing is, you're right. She is more yours than she has ever been anyone's. Karen trained her, a whole bunch of kids rode her before I was even born. She gave me an education...but..." he lost his flow here, "she's never been any one person's pony...*the* pony...until...until you came along. And I think...I think she feels it, too. And I don't know whether I am making the right decision here. Who am I to split you two up again? Who am I to take from her that chance of being someone's actual pony before she dies? - I was thinking about it all last night while I was watching you sleep."

He sighed deeply.

If Eleanor had had two hearts beating in her chest they would have been racing each other at this point. One for the idea that she could be Blue's one person, the other for the knowledge that he had watched her sleep. As it was, the one she did have felt like it was ready to burst, so much so that she found it almost impossible to speak. So she squished his hand, hard, and forced the words out against the noise of the blood rushing in her ears and against the part of her still fighting the inevitable, refusing to give up hope.

"You're doing the right thing."

Just then it came into view. They'd come around the bend in the road and there it was, parked up innocently outside the main entrance to Hawthorne Cottage: a big tatty red box lorry with 'Caution Horses' written on the ramp.

It was the second time in three days that she entered the house through the front door and as she went past him - holding the door open to her with a bow and a "Milady" in a feeble attempt to inject some comedy into the situation - she couldn't help feeling that somehow there was significance in that.

The house was quiet and dark, other than a faint light emanating from the kitchen. They silently made towards it.

The table, which had been brought back in along with the chairs, was set for eight people but only a solitary figure sat at the short end of the bench, head bent low so just the top of it could be seen, engrossed in a book and sipping tea from a mug beside her. She had practical, short black hair with silver streaks and from the hands turning the page Eleanor could see that her skin tone was much whiter than her nephew's, much more like her father's. The way she handled the book, too, reminded Eleanor of Aaron. The eyes that greeted them when she looked up were also a carbon copy of the old man's, steel grey with a black rim around the iris, which in combination with the distinctly Sioux bone structure and the black and silver hair around a young face, gave her a wolf-like appearance - not very pretty yet somehow fascinating to look at. She was a lot broader and more compact in stature than Eleanor had imagined her, too. All in all, she looked nothing like the Karen Eleanor had envisioned.

She felt right though. She didn't get up in a hurry, there were no Nice-to-meet-you-s or You-must-be-s, no introduction as such, just a broad smile and curiosity sparkling behind the eyes as she took a long but kind look at Eleanor before grinning up at her nephew.

"You're both here," she finally stated, "good. - Hi P."

"K," he nodded, "how was the journey?"

"Alright. Stopped over at Rachael's in Clipstone last night. Too much otherwise. Nice yard she's got there. Beautiful riding. You should go see her sometime."

If they shared nothing else, her patter, Eleanor realised, was exactly like his. They *sounded* like family.

Karen shut the book and got up. She was only about a foot taller than Eleanor and wearing the holey jumper that Eleanor had borrowed after the rains, weeks ago. Karen caught the girl looking at it and smiled, tugging at the garment.

"Found this on the landing. My favourite. I thought it had vanished in the move. You been wearing it?"

Eleanor nodded shyly.

"That's okay. I'm having it back though," she turned her attention back to the boy, "Now stop being a pillock and come here." She opened her arms.

As they hugged, Eleanor could see the love between them as if it was something tangible and she was about to respectfully retreat when Karen loosened one arm out of the hug and grabbed her by the sleeve.

"Where do you think you're going?" She untangled herself from the embrace and took a hand in each hand - girl to the right, boy to the left.

"Now, children," she grinned, "Come with me, I have something to show you."

As she dragged them behind her through the door, they shot each other a glance, raising eyebrows and shrugging in unison. Somehow, for the moment, their sadness was being drowned out by the excitement shooting directly from Karen's hands up into theirs.

"Where are we going?" Eleanor asked.

"The paddock."

"Where are grandpa and Sarah?" his turn.

"Out. Back in a bit."

"Why is the table laid for so many?"

"Ah, that would be telling."

Karen wouldn't answer any more questions, cryptically or not, as she pulled them through the back door and the garden, through the door in the wall, down the twitten and to the metal gate. There she let go of them and climbed to perch atop, bidding them to do the same. As they sat there like roosting chickens, all three scanned the land in front of them.

Blue was nowhere to be seen but that wasn't unusual since she had started favouring the paddock behind the barn of late. As Eleanor thought about it, the excitement she had siphoned off the woman next to her waned and she could start feeling the familiar lump of ice in her innards again.

A faint smile played around Karen's lips as she turned towards Eleanor with a wink and mouthed a "wait". The ability to pick up on Eleanor's thoughts seemed to run in the family, too. Karen turned to her nephew, lost in his own thoughts, top lip trembling.

"Right," she said authoritatively, "what's your name?"

"Do me a favour, auntie K."

"I am. - What's your name?"

"Paytah," he said with a sigh, "Paytah Hawthorne, third Earl of horseshit."

"Better," she grinned, "although it will still need some work. Now hop off, go into the paddock and whistle like you used to whistle for Inara."

He flinched when she said the dead mare's name but did as he was told.

The horse came flying out of nowhere.

A flash of brown, black and white, streaked mane fluttering in the wind, tail high up in the air, head held high. It looked younger than the mare in the picture, not quite finished yet but at the same time more strongly built, like one day it would become a powerhouse of muscles and legs.

A boy horse, Eleanor thought. *The boy horse.*

The colt had stopped some paces away from the boy, eyeing him up. She couldn't hear what he was saying but heard a low murmur and the colt answered him back with an equally low nicker in his throat. She saw him put out his hand, palm up and the horse stepping towards it, arching his long neck and sniffing it. Eleanor half expected for a dance to ensue, like the one she'd gone through with Blue when they'd first met but things between these two entities were much quicker and clearer, much more immediate. After sniffing the boy's hand the colt suddenly darted forward and began rubbing his forehead against the boy's chest then snuck his head around to his side and back to rub his cheeks against those. The boy laughed, slung his arms around the horse's neck and it rubbed its jaw against his shoulder.

Back on the gate Karen gently nudged Eleanor who was watching in wonder.

"And to think some people will punish their horses for doing that," the older woman said quietly, "Idiots. They blabber about lack of respect and personal space - and have no idea. They don't get the difference between a pack and a herd. In Arabian countries the men will encourage this behaviour. They see it as meaning the stallion sees you as his master. Equally idiotic, but much closer to the truth."

"It's belonging, isn't it?" Eleanor whispered insecurely, "Being together."

Karen cocked her head and narrowed her eyes at the girl, a small smile curling up her lips as she nodded almost imperceptibly. Then she laughed.

"It's having a good old snuggle, is what it is. You just have to teach them not to be as rough with you as they can be with each other. Our skin's a lot thinner," she turned back to the boy and the colt, "Right, you two, enough of that. Come hither!"

They came, together, horse following boy like a dog, until the boy came to stand before the gate and the horse sauntered off. Looking up at his aunt, the boy's eyes suddenly darkened.

"Why is he here?" he asked harshly, "What did you bring him for?"

"Well, you see, it's like this," Karen answered matter-of-factly, "there is no place for a tri-coloured sexually mature colt at a stud farm that wants to exclusively breed Fales or Driesians. It's too much of a risk and too much of a headache. So I have a choice. Have him gelded or find him a home where he can remain whole and become the beautiful stallion he will be. I'd prefer the latter. He's the last of the Wachiwi line that we know of. She would be turning in her grave if we had him chopped. So, I put my feelers out and it seems like the Wachiwi name still carries quite a bit of clout down here. There are a couple of people very interested in continuing the line. Prepared to pay good money for him, too."

If over the last couple of months Eleanor had seen those amber eyes go all shades of yellow, red and mahogany with a myriad of sparks going off, she had never seen anger like this in him before. It was as if somebody had set a whole fireworks factory alight. He was shaking, skin ashen, fists clenched, hardly able to speak – glaring at his aunt as if she were the devil herself.

Karen didn't flinch.

"You are not selling one of ours," he pressed out from in between clenched teeth, "Over my dead body. He's not yours to sell anyway. He's Inara's son, so he's mine. If you can't keep him up there, he's staying with me. Period. I've got till Monday, I'll figure something out. The Richards have space and only geldings, I'm sure they'll give me free livery in return for lessons and some help. If not, I'll put him and Blue in the garden for all I care. She is too old to conceive, they'll be fine. They're not going anywhere."

There was moment of complete silence before Karen's poker face melted into a smile that would have tugged at the heart strings of even the most hard-nosed person on the planet.

"Is the correct answer," she stated, before cupping her nephew's face in her hands and kissing him square on the mouth, "welcome back to the world, P."

Then she withdrew, gesturing for them to hang on a minute and fished her phone out of her pocket. Her call was answered immediately.

"Go ahead," was all she said but didn't hang up for a while, nodding with satisfaction before finishing on, "I'll see you in half an hour or so."

She hung up, put the phone away and dug out a bunch of keys. She detached a separate ring with two keys from the bundle and looked at Eleanor.

"Open hand," she said simply.

Eleanor complied. The keys dropped in her hand.

"One for the barn and one for the padlock on the gate." She looked from boy to girl and back, clearly enjoying their confusion. Finally she added, "P meet your new landlady."

Chapter 37

"I so want to be a fly on the wall and see his stupid face when he checks his bank balance and finds it's all there," Charly said for the umpteenth time before grabbing another bread roll and cutting it open.

"Well, you could have stayed around till tonight if you had wanted to," Karen who was sitting next to her, replied while cutting a tomato into slices on her plate, knife dragging against the china, making Isabel and Kjell cringe in unison a few seats down.

"What and risk him trying to stop me from taking Ravenna and Casta?" Charly asked. She had arrived last in the breakfast round, having come to get the horsebox first, only to return an hour or so later with Casta as well as her own mare and all her and their belongings on board. She'd been a bit worse for wear when she'd first turned up after a long night with Ebony but was picking up now with every cup of coffee and every one of the numerous rolls that were disappearing at an alarming rate through her gargantuan lips. "I'm no idiot. He's gonna have baby pumas when he finds out and I don't want to be in his firing line when he does. I reckon he's coming back from the auction at around five, I want to be the other side of the Watford Gap by then, pretty please. We're leaving after lunch, right?" She was looking imploringly at Karen. Karen nodded and sighed.

"I'd have liked to have stayed a bit longer," she looked at Paytah and Eleanor who'd pretty much finished eating and were huddled together on the long side of the bench, happy but still stunned and incredulous at the turn of events, "I would have liked to get to know you a bit, Eleanor," she smiled sadly at the girl and shrugged, "That's the drawback of being the only groom in a place but that's going to change," she nudged Charly, "so in the future I can actually come and visit from time to time. So next time, eh? Or maybe you could come up and see us one day. I miss you." Her eyes wandered back and forth between her nephew and her father, sitting at the other end of the table.

Just then Sarah returned from the barn where she'd been checking on her mare. Aaron looked up at his friend enquiringly. She made a so-so gesture with her hands. "She'll be fine. It'll be better once Ravenna is gone, so we can let the three of them out and they can start sorting themselves into an order. Although I dare say you should look for a livery as soon as. Three is not a good number," the last part was aimed at Eleanor who suddenly felt very small and childlike, looking around the grown up's faces in wonder and amazement.

While she and the boy next to her had been fretting and dying inside, the adults had been plotting. Plotting like Eleanor had never realised people could plot outside of eight-year-olds playing make believe – and that's what they all felt like right now. Like a bunch of children who'd hatched a wild, impossible plan and had somehow pulled it off.

"I agree," interjected Kjell thoughtfully, while lovingly arranging ham and salad on his roll, "two is company, three is a crowd, four is a herd."

"It would have to be a gelding though, so we don't have any surprise additions next year," Paytah pondered, "but it would have to be something small so Inigo doesn't see him as a threat but as back up."

Karen murmured in agreement while chewing on a piece of cheese, then looked at Sarah to once more ask the same question she'd asked a few times today already.

"And you are absolutely sure your mare is barren?"

It obviously worried her. Sarah and Casta had been an unexpected variable in the equation and it made her uneasy, despite Aaron's musings that surprise twists, if they improved upon a plan, only served to verify the brilliance of the plan in the first place.

Sarah shrugged, giving her the same answer she'd given previously.

"She ran with a most prolific Spanish stallion for six years and no foal. Sad really, I think she would have made a fine mother."

Just then Oscar piped up from the car seat on the floor, where he'd been asleep.

"Speaking of motherhood," Isabel said before she put the last bit of a boiled egg in her mouth, made her excuses and grabbed the baby to go and feed him in another room.

Eleanor's eyes followed her mum out. She didn't want her excluded. Her, the woman who at the end of the day had made it all happen, who had saved the day and the land - with allegedly only a tiny bit of persuasion from Kjell. She wriggled out from under Paytah's arm and searched his eyes. He understood.

She slipped from the bench and crawled under the table so as not to disturb the round too much, emerged on the other side next to Kjell who smiled as she appeared and made her way to the sitting room.

She found her mum sitting on one of the four assorted period style sofas that dominated this room. Oscar was suckling happily on a breast while Isabel seemed to contemplate the large black-and-white engraving that hung over the fire place, 'The Widow of an Indian Chief Watching the Arms of Her Deceased Husband'.

"I didn't realise there was an engraving of this. I saw the painting, you know, in Derby museum. Years ago…funny, I remember standing in front of it, thinking it was somehow going to be important…" Isabel's voice trailed off.

Eleanor gently sat down next to her mum on the sofa.

"Thank you, mum."

Isabel looked at her sideways.

"What for?"

"You know what."

Isabel shrugged and looked down at the baby's face, gently stroking its cheek with the back of her finger as it drank in big gulps.

"You were never this greedy, you know. I had a real nightmare getting you to latch on. My little fidgety bag of skin and bones…" her voice trailed off again, then gathered conviction, "It's your money, Eleanor. And Kjell is right. Whatever happens here, with you two and those ponies, investing in land is always infinitely preferable to having money in the bank. - It just makes me sad to think that you'd ask Jerry but not me."

Eleanor swallowed hard. Even as she had made that phone call, sometime between midnight and dawn during the longest night of her life, she'd known it would come back to bite her.

"I didn't think we had the money, mum."

"I always said *Kittens in the Den* was yours."

"Yeah, but I never thought you meant *literally.* Or that it had earned so much over the years."

Isabel smiled, a mixture of mischief and sadness.

"It's done pretty well, that little ditty we wrote, hasn't it?" Isabel had always maintained that she had been nothing but the lesser partner in conceiving her most famous piece; that it had been a collaboration written mostly by the restless soul she had harboured in her belly at the time.

"You know," she said looking at her daughter again, whose appearance had gone almost completely feral over a summer spent outdoors and in the wilderness of first love, making her look more like the sprite she proclaimed to be than ever and suppressed a laugh, "there is even enough money left over for a haircut before school starts."

2401594R00140

Printed in Germany
by Amazon Distribution
GmbH, Leipzig